Abducted

Bill Ward

CHAPTER ONE

Powell was on a morning flight to Bucharest, uncertain if he was going to be able to locate Dimitry, who he was intent on eliminating. Powell was assuming the role of human pest controller. Dimitry had murdered his daughter and Powell believed eliminating was the correct word to describe his intentions towards Dimitry. He didn't think of it in terms of murder, although the authorities would consider it so, but of removing a vile and evil menace, who had repeatedly proven he did not deserve to live.

Powell stretched his legs and was grateful for the aisle seat, as at six feet two inches tall, any other seat made flying a difficult experience, especially travelling economy class. It had been a life changing few weeks, in which he had lost his daughter Bella, stabbed to death on a Brighton street by Dimitry. She was a fledgling police officer and had stumbled across a young Romanian girl called Afina, who was fleeing from Dimitry's clutches. Afina was of a similar age to his daughter and had been trafficked into Brighton by Dimitry and his friends, to work as a sex slave.

Powell had helped Afina escape and temporarily forge a new life but Dimitry was not willing to leave alive a witness to his murderous actions. He had repeatedly threatened the lives of Afina's mother and sister, leaving Powell with no option but to take action.

Powell had grown close to Afina and her family, and made Afina a promise before leaving England, he would only return once her family's safety was assured. He was a man who always kept his promises and the only possible way to guarantee that safety was to eliminate Dimitry.

That Powell was able to contemplate terminating Dimitry's life, was the result of his having worked for MI5 in his twenties, when he was a field operative used to dangerous situations and the need to terminate with extreme prejudice. That had been the in vogue terminology in those days, which now seemed a bit of a bizarre way of describing government authorised assassination.

At least the intensive training he'd received in the distant past was paying off. Although twenty years away from the business, Powell had recently discovered he had lost none of his capabilities. In fact, having become a

3

second Dan black belt in kickboxing, his skills had probably increased not waned over the years.

What had changed was his views on the use of extreme force. It no longer came as second nature to end the life of any human being and in the case of Dimitry, it was very much a last resort, when all other attempts to keep within the law had failed.

Powell spent some of the flight thinking about his feelings for Afina. She was twenty two so at forty nine years of age, Powell was old enough to be her father and then some. Their relationship had kicked off in an unconventional manner, with his pretending to be someone called Danny and paying her to have sex, in the early days of his search for Dimitry. Despite the strange beginning, Afina had recently suggested by way of some passionate kisses that she wanted more from him than friendship. He was still undecided. There was a definite physical attraction on his part and he also admired her courage but there were lingering doubts about their age difference in particular.

She would surely want children at some point and he could not contemplate starting a new family. Neither did he want a few good years with her only to then be kicked into touch for someone younger, as the age difference became too great an obstacle. She would still be in her thirties when he was drawing a pension!

There was also a part of Powell which was reluctant to allow anyone to get too close. After the death of his daughter and in danger of wallowing in self-pity, Powell had made the decision to assist those whom the law had failed, in order to give some meaning and direction to his life. It was his way of honouring his daughter's memory. It would undoubtedly be necessary sometimes to take the law into his own hands, which would be dangerous for him and potentially anyone close to him.

Powell was keen not to spend too much time finding Dimitry, as he had postponed a meeting with Angela Bennett, who was seeking his help with recovering her children from her ex-husband in Saudi Arabia. Abdullah Rashid had married Bennett while working at the Saudi embassy in London and they had been married for eleven years when he took the children to Saudi Arabia, for their annual visit to his parents. The day before he was due to return, he had phoned her to say neither he or the children would be returning to the UK. The children would be living with him in future.

She had tried the legal route to gain access to her children but despite the

English Courts ruling in her favour, they had no jurisdiction in Saudi Arabia, where thy didn't recognise the rights of a mother or it appeared, women in general. Desperate to reclaim her children and having exhausted all other possibilities, she had turned to Powell for assistance. The Bennett woman seemed like a prime candidate to help but first he needed to dispose of Dimitry.

CHAPTER TWO

Powell had booked into the same hotel as on his previous visit to Bucharest and though it was late, he decided he would visit Dimitry's club. He had gone over in his mind every detail of the events since he had last seen Dimitry and reasoned there should be no solid reason for Dimitry not to still believe he was Danny and could be trusted.

Danny had been the pseudonym Powell used to befriend Dimitry, infiltrating his sex trafficking organisation and leading him into the trap, which led to his arrest. However, Powell had ensured it looked as if Danny had simply been lucky and escaped arrest. The only problem would be if Dimitry had spoken with his friend Victor, in the small window of time after escaping from prison and before Powell strangled the life out of Victor. It seemed unlikely as Dimitry would have been preoccupied with fleeing the country. It was a risk Powell was prepared to take and in any event he still intended to be very cautious.

It was undoubtedly Dimitry's absurd perception that all his misfortune was due to Afina, rather than his own actions, which was why he had gone after her family. Powell knew there was nothing subtle about Dimitry. Someone had upset him so he was prepared to go to any lengths for revenge. In some ways, as an adversary, it made him easier to read and predictable.

He would have heard about the death of Victor, at the hands of the father of the policewoman he'd killed, but there were no photos of Powell anywhere on the internet to identify him as the same person Dimitry knew as Danny. Powell had never used any of the social media sites, which all involved adding photos or profiles, just in case someone from his past still wanted to locate him. In fact, he had always been averse generally to appearing in photos.

His days in MI5 had created enemies and there were men who would be happy to see him dead. There was no point in making it easy for them to find him. Bella thought he was old fashioned and anti-technology but really he was just being cautious.

Powell was certainly apprehensive as the taxi dropped him off at the end of the street. He'd thought through what he was going to say if Dimitry was in the club but considered it more likely he was hiding somewhere else. Surely if he was at his club the local police would have arrested him by now, as an international warrant for his arrest had been issued.

Powell walked slowly, hoping the promise he would always be welcome at the club, still held good. He stood in the doorway and looked around to see who was present and barely had time to take in the scene when the friendly bouncer with the goatee beard, who he remembered from his previous visit, came rushing up.

"Danny, it's good to see you again. No one told me you were coming."

"Actually, I'm not expected. I just came by on the off chance Dimitry was here."

The bouncer looked around as if checking no one could overhear their conversation. He leaned in closer and spoke quietly. "I'm afraid he's not here now but he was earlier. He's keeping a low profile."

"Can someone let him know I'm here? I have no way of contacting him." Powell had a mobile number from Dimitry's time in Brighton but wasn't really surprised it no longer worked.

"Come downstairs and have a drink. Bogdan is here and he will be able to get a message to Dimitry."

Powell followed him down the stairs to the private part of the club where lap dancing was available, hoping he wasn't walking into a trap. He recognised Bogdan sitting with a couple of other men he didn't know.

"Look who is here," the bouncer announced.

"Danny, it is good to see you again," Bogdan said warmly, having taken a second to register the presence of Powell. "This is a big surprise."

Powell was happy with the friendly greeting. It augured well for Dimitry not having discovered the truth. "Good to see you again, Bogdan. Life in Brighton was becoming too dangerous so I could think of nowhere better to visit for a holiday, until it calms down back home."

"As you probably know, Dimitry also had problems in England."

"Yes, I was with him when he was arrested. I only just managed to escape."

"You were lucky."

"I think it was Dimitry they really wanted. I am just a small fish by comparison."

"I will see Dimitry tomorrow morning and tell him you are here."

"I'm staying at the Grand hotel again so ask him to give me a call and we can arrange to meet."

"I will. He left earlier with a couple of girls, otherwise I would call him now but I don't think he wants to be disturbed," Bogdan explained, smiling broadly. "We must have a drink. What would you like?"

"I'll have a shot of Tuica and a beer, please." Powell had grown quite attached to the national drink of Tuica on his last visit. Made from plums it tasted a bit like vodka.

Bogdan pulled up a chair for Powell and signalled for a waitress to take their order. "Would you like some girls for tonight?" he asked.

"Not tonight thanks. I'm very tired, which also means I'm just going to have a couple of drinks and then get some sleep. Perhaps tomorrow we can party properly?"

CHAPTER THREE

Powell awoke at seven and ate a large breakfast. He could imagine how the condemned man felt who ordered his last meal. He would soon find out whether or not Dimitry considered him a friend. He tried to keep negative thoughts from his mind and put in a call to Afina to let her know everything was progressing positively, at least for the time being. She had made him promise to keep in regular contact as otherwise she would fear the worst.

He doubted he would hear from Dimitry very early so he intended to spend some time on his laptop, researching the Bennett case. One of the factors which had so far stopped him finally committing to help Angela Bennett, was his lack of knowledge about the Middle East in general and Saudi Arabia in particular. He only knew what he occasionally read in the newspapers and most of that simply focused on the latest atrocity committed by ISIS. He wanted to learn more about everyday life.

It was mid-morning when Powell heard from Dimitry, who suggested they meet for some lunch. Dimitry was friendly and Powell could detect no obvious cause for concern in either what he said or his tone of voice. Then again, if Dimitry was setting a trap, it was exactly how he would want to come across on the phone. Powell was going to tread warily, he had no weapon or backup so would need to stay alert. At least Dimitry was not aware of his kickboxing skills.

Powell was waiting in the hotel reception when Dimitry entered.

"Good to see you, Danny," Dimitry said with a broad smile.

"And you, Dimitry," Powell replied, shaking hands. "You look very different." Dimitry's full beard had been replaced by just a stubble.

"I thought it best to change my appearance when I escaped from your English courtroom. The beard was too recognisable."

"So where do you suggest we eat? Much as I love your club, somewhere different would be good. I haven't seen much of your city." Powell was keen not to have lunch on Dimitry's home territory, surrounded by his henchmen.

"I know a very nice restaurant not far from here. It serves very good Romanian food and has an excellent selection of Tuica! We can get drunk and celebrate our good fortune to escape your English police."

"Sounds like a great idea," Powell agreed. He had no intention of getting drunk but would welcome Dimitry having an excess of alcohol, which might inhibit his reactions.

Dimitry led the way back out to his Mercedes and climbed in the driver's seat. "I didn't think you could drive," Powell joked. Dimitry had always previously used a driver. "Where is Bogdan today?"

"He had some family business that needed his attention. Anyway, I like to drive sometimes."

"Driving has lost all pleasure in England, there are too many traffic cameras and restrictions."

"We are lucky, we don't have many cameras in Romania. The best driving though is on the German autobahns. That can be real fun."

Powell wondered if Dimitry planned to still drive after lunch, when he would inevitably be drunk. Powell would insist on taking a taxi back to the hotel even if it caused offence. He wasn't going to end up as a traffic accident statistic in a foreign country.

During the ten minute journey, Dimitry recounted how he escaped from the courtroom and returned to Romania. He had taken the Eurostar to Paris and then a flight to Bucharest using a false passport.

"Within twenty four hours of appearing in your court, I was back here drinking a cold beer."

"And a few Tuicas, no doubt."

"Yes, it was a good night and after a few drinks, I may tell you about the pleasure I had with three very beautiful young girls."

"Three? You are a greedy man, Dimitry." Powell couldn't think of anything worse than hearing about Dimitry's excesses and how he had mistreated some unfortunate girls.

"We are men. What else are we to do? I did the girls a service, introducing them to what real men enjoy. It will serve them well in later life when they are trying to keep their husbands satisfied."

"I'm sure their husbands will be eternally grateful." Powell wondered if Dimitry really believed the crap he uttered.

They parked and two minutes later arrived outside a restaurant called Arcade Cafe. Powell realised they were in the centre of the old town so probably not far from Dimitry's club.

"This is a fun place in the evenings," Dimitry revealed. "They always have Karaoke and it's a great place to find girls."

As Dimitry led the way into the café, Powell found himself in a very atmospheric lounge area. As well as the wrought iron chairs and wooden tables, there were chandeliers, lamps and paintings creating a warm environment. Powell could tell the café had a vibe which would attract the young and make it a hunting ground for Dimitry and his friends.

Dimitry led the way downstairs to a large restaurant and bar area with sofas, bookcases and more vintage paintings on the brick walls. It was definitely trendy and quite unique.

"I hope you're hungry," Dimitry said, once they were seated. "They do a great steak."

"I could eat a horse," Powell replied.

"I don't think they have horse on the menu," Dimitry replied with a grin.

"In that case I'll have a steak as well."

Food and drinks were ordered and then Dimitry asked, "How long do you plan to stay in Bucharest?"

"I'm not sure but at least a few days. I can't go back to Brighton easily so when I do go back, I will probably head for London. Or maybe I will go somewhere hot for a year like Spain."

"I don't think I will be visiting England again for a very long time," Dimitry voiced with an air of resignation. "Pity because I really like England."

"By the way, how is Stefan?" Powell inquired.

"He is bored waiting for his trial but he will be found not guilty."

Powell was surprised by Dimitry's confidence about the outcome of the trial. "The police must have several witnesses. Why are you so sure he will be found not guilty?"

"We will have words with the girls and their families. They won't testify. And for insurance we will pay some of the jurors to make the right decision."

"Good. I like Stefan." Powell wondered if Dimitry would really find it as easy as he thought to manipulate Stefan's trial. He was going to have to warn the police.

The waitress delivered their drinks and Powell wasn't altogether surprised to see Dimitry had ordered a bottle of Tuica not just a glass each.

"To Stefan," Powell toasted.

"Stefan," Dimitry responded touching glasses.

They downed their shots in one and Dimitry quickly poured refills. As he raised his glass to propose another toast, his phone rang. He looked at the number and answered, "Hello Bogdan." Then he listened for a minute before saying, "Good." He returned the phone to his pocket and once again raised his glass. "Tonight you must again be my guest at the club for dinner and after I am going to provide some special entertainment."

Powell thought it highly likely the entertainment would include some girls. He needed to get Dimitry on his own or at least away from the likes of Bogdan, he wondered if this entertainment would afford the opportunity.

After a great meal, Powell declined Dimitry's offer of a lift back to his hotel, saying he needed to stretch his legs and wanted to have a look around the old town. In truth he didn't want Dimitry driving him anywhere after the quantity of alcohol he had consumed. Powell would love to turn up at the club in the evening and discover Dimitry had been killed in an accident. That would make life so much easier.

Once Dimitry had driven off, Powell ordered a taxi to take him back to his hotel. Once back inside his room, Powell checked the drawers and cupboards. There was no doubt someone had been inside his room and searched his belongings. Fortunately, it was someone who didn't have the experience to identify the small traps he had left, which showed his clothes had been moved.

Was it Bogdan? Did that explain his earlier absence? Powell hoped it was just a case of Dimitry being cautious rather than having any concrete reasons for suspecting him. In any event, there was nothing incriminating in his room. Powell hoped Dimitry would be satisfied with the results of the search. He didn't want to be walking into a trap when they met again for dinner.

CHAPTER FOUR

Powell had dinner at Dimitry's club with Bogdan and a couple of other heavyset types, who looked and sounded like they had more muscle than brains. Dimitry was a good host and provided excessive amounts of alcohol, which Powell pretended to drink heavily but in reality he was consuming a fraction of what the others drank.

A couple of girls Powell hadn't seen before, performed a strip for the table but Dimitry promised the entertainment he had organised for later would be far more exciting. Powell realised he could shortly be facing a difficult dilemma because he was not going to just stand by and witness the terrible abuse of any girl. If it cost him his life so be it but he would have surprise on his side and he intended to unleash a terrible fury, which he had been suppressing since his daughter's death.

About eleven, Dimitry announced it was time for the entertainment and he led the way to the back of the basement room where they had been eating, through a door and along a corridor to a small room where chairs were placed around the edge of the room, surrounding a small circular stage. To one side was a small bar. Powell had a horrible feeling it was something akin to a miniature arena, of the sort where, in Roman times, gladiatorial combat was provided as entertainment for the bloodthirsty masses.

"Take a chair, Danny," Dimitry suggested. "The fun will start in a few minutes. This is where we have our special parties. The room is sound proofed so we are never disturbed."

Powell realised the two heavies hadn't joined them. Bogdan poured some drinks from behind the bar and handed one to Powell.

The sound of the door opening made Powell turn around and he saw a young girl, probably no more than sixteen years old, pushed into the room followed by the two heavies. The girl's hair was dishevelled and mascara smudged around her eyes where she had been crying. She stumbled as she received a further push from behind. Powell turned away shocked. How had they found Afina's sister? She was supposed to be staying with a friend.

Powell knew he had to act immediately. Once on stage and facing him, she would recognise him and in her desperate state might ruin everything. He walked quickly to the girl and put his arms around her, keeping his back between her and the others so they didn't see her reaction, he leaned in close as if to kiss her.

"Adriana, it's me, Powell," he said quietly. "Don't say anything. I'll get you out of here."

She blinked to clear her eyes and then seeing it was him, her eyes lit up with hope.

"This is going to be fun," Powell stated. "I don't suppose you'd let me have her all to myself for a bit?"

"Now you are being greedy," Dimitry answered. "This girl is the sister of that damned Afina and we are all going to share in the fun. You gave me the idea Danny, when you talked about making special films. We are going to make a film here and send it to that bitch Afina as a present. She will learn what it means to fuck with me."

"On the stage," Powell demanded. "You can start by dancing for us." He thought it was the safest place for her to be for the next few minutes.

"You can direct our film a little if you wish," Dimitry said.

"I would love that. How old is she?" Powell asked.

"Sweet sixteen and though I doubt she is a virgin, I'm sure she won't have experienced anything like we have planned for her," Dimitry laughed.

"Well I've heard some interesting stories about the size of your cock, Dimitry. I look forward to seeing it in action."

"Whichever woman said size doesn't matter had never had my cock in her arse!" Dimitry laughed.

Powell had been willing to sacrifice his own life, if he could be sure of killing Dimitry but seeing Adriana gave him a whole new responsibility. For Afina's sake he had to save her sister. It was even more important than his revenge.

Powell needed to improve the odds. He doubted his ability to take down all four men in the room. He pretended to search his pockets. "I would like my own personal film of this but I seem to have left my phone back where we ate. Could someone get it for me?"

"Of course," Dimitry responded quickly. He said something in Romanian and one of the heavies left the room.

Powell downed his drink in one and walked towards the bar. "I think I'll have another of those, please."

As he passed the remaining heavy, he delivered a vicious blow with the side of his left hand to the man's throat. The others in the room seemed to freeze, not quite understanding what had just happened. In those seconds, Powell delivered a kick to Bogdan's crutch, which caused him to bend double in agony. The follow up round house kick to the jaw sent him crashing to the floor unconscious.

The heavy was gripping his throat, seeking some way to alleviate the pain and lack of oxygen entering his lungs but still managed a lunge towards Powell, who easily avoided the flailing fist. Powell used the heavy's forward motion against him by using his foot to sweep away the man's legs, leaving the man's weight and gravity to send him to join Bogdan on the floor. Powell delivered a further kick to the side of the head and the man stopped moving.

"Powell, he has a knife," Adriana shouted.

Powell turned quickly to face Dimitry, who had a large knife in his hand.

Dimitry looked from Adriana to Powell with a quizzical look on his face. "So you two know each other? Why did she call you Powell?"

"It's my name. It was also the name of the young police officer you killed in Brighton. She was my daughter."

Dimitry took a few seconds to understand what he had heard then a small smile crossed his lips. "So Bogdan was right not to trust you. I assume you are responsible for the death of Victor and Stefan being in prison?" Dimitry was circling Powell, brandishing the large knife, looking for an opening.

Powell realised Dimitry was also trying to buy time until the heavy returned to announce he couldn't find the phone that was inside his jacket pocket all the time.

Powell had to force the issue. "Enough of talking," he said. "It is time for you to pay for your crimes."

Powell feinted to the left with his fist as if to throw a punch but in the same movement he kicked out with his right foot and landed a severe blow on Dimitry's left kneecap, which caused him to immediately drop his knife and cry out in excruciating pain. Powell had herd the crack and knew his blow had disabled Dimitry.

For the first time, Powell saw a look of fear on Dimitry's face. There was perspiration on his forehead. Gone was his normal confidence. He tried to back away but his broken knee made it impossible for him to do anything except a slow shuffle.

Dimitry shouted out something unintelligible in Romanian, which Powell reckoned was a cry for help. He had obviously forgotten his earlier proud announcement of how the room was completely sound proofed.

Dimitry was having to use his one good leg to support all his weight so when Powell delivered a kick to the good knee it was even more devastating. Dimitry howled and fell backwards to the floor.

Powell picked up the knife from the floor and advanced on Dimitry. "I genuinely wish I could spend more time with you but I need to get Adriana safely away from here so this will have to be quick."

Dimitry had his hands up in front of him in a useless attempt to defend himself. "I can make you very rich," he begged.

"You honestly think I would take your money made from trafficking girls, in return for letting you live?" He was close enough to step on Dimitry's knee and the resulting scream he emitted was terrible. "You have blighted the lives of too many young women. No amount of money can bring back my daughter."

Adriana moved close to where Dimitry lay and spat at him. "You fucking pig," she swore.

As Dimitry was distracted by a further rant in Romanian from Adriana, with a swift movement Powell buried the knife deep in Dimitry's chest. There was no joy in Powell's heart at ending a life, no great feeling of revenge, just the thought it was fitting that the man who had lived by the knife and stabbed Bella to death, should also die by the knife.

Powell didn't have long to dwell on the thought. A second later the door was opened and in walked the heavy. He stopped and surveyed the room as Powell withdrew the knife from Dimitry's body and turned in his direction.

"Do you understand some English?" Powell asked.

"A little."

"You now have to decide whether you live or die today. If you feel any duty to your dead boss and come at me, you will end up like your friends." He let his words sink in for a second then continued, "I am leaving now with the girl."

Powell took Adriana by the hand and led her towards the door. The heavy stood in the way but after a second's thought moved aside and let them pass.

Powell didn't head back in the direction of the club but towards the door he had spotted in the other direction, at the end of the corridor. He pushed on the bar and they were out on a side street he didn't recognise.

"We need to hurry," Powell encouraged, pulling on Adriana's arm. "Just in case they have further backup nearby."

"Where are we going?"

"As far away from here as possible."

CHAPTER FIVE

Powell took a risk by going back to his hotel and checking out but reasoned with Dimitry dead, there would be no one to quickly take charge and come looking for him. He didn't want to leave all his possessions behind if it wasn't absolutely necessary and more importantly, Adriana needed the chance to clean herself up. With her smudged mascara and torn clothes she looked as if she had taken grunge style to a whole new level.

While Powell packed, Adriana took the quickest ever shower. Without makeup she looked a lot fresher and younger. Powell provided a clean t-shirt and they headed downstairs to the taxi rank in front of the hotel.

"Where is your passport?" Powell asked, once they were both sat in the back seat of the taxi.

"Why do I need my passport? I am not going with you. I must stay and look after my mother."

"Adriana, your life is in danger. Next time I may not be here to save you."

"You think there will be a next time? Surely now Dimitry is dead it is finished?"

"Probably but Bogdan and the others might come looking for you."

"I will find somewhere new to stay but I am not leaving."

"You are as obstinate as your big sister."

The taxi driver said something in Romanian. He sounded irritated.

"He wants to know where we are going," Adriana translated.

"The airport."

"But I told you I will not go with you."

Powell raised his finger to his lips. "I understand but we still need the airport. Just trust me, I have an idea. Tell him we're in a hurry."

Adriana said something to the driver and he accelerated away like a motor racing driver.

The taxi driver insisted on talking to them in animated fashion during the journey, despite Powell not understanding anything. Every so often Adriana would say something short, which would be followed by another long tirade from the driver. Powell doubted he was missing much by not understanding the language.

More than once, the driver would take both his hands off the steering wheel to emphasize a point and Powell began to worry it was a less than fifty, fifty chance whether they made it to the airport alive.

The driver dropped them at departures and seemed very happy with his large tip. Powell knew it was a large enough tip that should someone ask questions he would remember the two fares who tipped so well.

Powell led the way to arrivals, where he found a desk selling rooms in various hotels. He picked a hotel on the outskirts of the city and then they exited the airport like any new arrivals and took a taxi to the hotel.

"If Dimitry's friends pursue us, they will hopefully think we have caught a plane," Powell explained.

Ideally, he would have been on the first plane back to England but Adriana was not going to budge. This left him with no choice but to ensure Adriana's safety before leaving.

Once in their new hotel room, he had learned from Adriana that she was snatched off the street by two men and bundled into the back of a car, a couple of hours before her appearance at the club. The adult friend where she was staying had gone out for the evening and bored, Adriana had walked to the local shop to buy some snacks.

The men had taken her back to the club and she had been locked in a small room.

"Did they hurt you?" Powell asked.

"Not really. One man slapped me to stop me screaming and they were pushing and shoving me but that was all… They didn't rape me, if that is what you wanted to know? I heard Dimitry tell his men not to touch me. He said they would get their chance later."

It was what he had wanted to know and he was relieved. "I guess they were saving you for my entertainment."

Adriana started shaking like a leaf and burst into tears. "What would they have done to me if you hadn't saved me?" She was suffering from delayed shock at the realisation of how much worse her ordeal could have been.

Powell put his arms around her and comforted her. "You're okay now," he assured her. "You're safe. Don't dwell on what might have been. You were very brave and between us we taught them a lesson."

After a minute she was calm and he released her from the hug.

"Are you hungry?" he asked.

"Starving."

"There was a machine in the hall selling drinks, crisps, etcetera." He rummaged in his pockets and found some coins. "Get yourself something. I'll have a coke."

Powell called his friend Brian in England, who held a senior position in MI5, the British Security Service where Powell had also once worked. Brian was Bella's godfather and a very old friend, who Powell had recently been asking for an increasing number of favours.

"I need the name of someone in the Romanian police or security services we can trust, to help protect Adriana and sort out this mess," he said, once he'd explained the night's events.

"Don't ask much in the middle of the night, do you? Okay, I'll get right on it and be back in touch as soon as possible."

"Thanks, Brian."

"Well done, by the way," Brian added. "On getting rid of that animal Dimitry. A great many girls will be able to sleep safer as a result."

Next, Powell phoned Afina and informed her he was with Adriana and she was safe, although Afina had been unaware she was ever in danger. When Powell briefly recounted the night's events to Afina and confirmed Dimitry would never again be a threat, he could hear the tears at the other end of the phone.

The sisters spoke for a few minutes in Romanian and then Adriana handed the phone back to Powell.

"I can never repay you for what you have done for me and my family," Afina said.

"Your thanks is sufficient payment. I did it for Bella and for all the girls ever trafficked by Dimitry and his evil friends."

Powell kept the call short as he was expecting to hear back from Brian.

Adriana managed to get a few hours of sleep while Powell stayed awake to keep watch, just in case of danger. In the early hours of the morning he finally had a call from someone senior in Romania's police, specifically targeted to combat sex trafficking. Arrangements were made for the officer to collect Adriana and escort her to a safe location. Powell would have preferred to keep Adriana close to him but Brian trusted this man and Powell trusted Brian.

When the officer arrived, Powell provided a brief statement of the evening's events. The officer had the best possible witness in Adriana and so had agreed Powell could fly back to England. Powell promised to be available to answer any further questions and to return to Romania if necessary.

Back at his bar in Brighton, Powell did his best to assure Afina that her sister was truly safe, although she wasn't easily convinced and seemed a little irked at Powell for not having brought Adriana with him, even if it meant dragging her screaming through customs.

Powell genuinely believed that with the death of Dimitry, Afina and her family were no longer in danger. It was Dimitry who Afina had seen murder Bella and his personal vendetta ended with his death.

A few hours later, Afina was able to speak with her sister and learned she was indeed safe, which led to her suggesting opening a bottle of champagne to celebrate. Powell went to the wine cellar and personally chose two bottles of an expensive pink Prosecco. He recalled Victor being locked in the metal inner cellar where the best wines were kept and smiled at the realisation the task he had set himself to revenge Bella, was at an end. Dimitry and Victor were both dead. Stefan was going to be spending a very long time behind bars. As he returned upstairs he felt more at peace than for a long time.

CHAPTER SIX

Powell had arranged to meet Angela Bennett at her home on the outskirts of Kingston upon Thames. The drive from Brighton took just over an hour and he was grateful for his car's navigation system, as he would otherwise have soon been lost in the town's one way system. The home was a substantial detached house in a quiet road full of imposing and undoubtedly very expensive houses.

The woman who opened the door was in her forties and attractive in an elegant sort of way, almost certainly revealing an upper class upbringing and money to spend on the best hairdressers and designer fashions. She was tall and slim with auburn hair cut in a bob. The overall look was feminine but despite the makeup, Powell could see the dark patches under the eyes, which suggested Angela Bennett wasn't sleeping well.

"It's so good to meet you," Angela greeted him with a warm smile.

Powell shook hands and followed her through to a lounge with expensive furnishings and accepted the offer of coffee. As he waited for her to return with the coffee, he looked at the various pictures on the walls, which he assumed were of her children and the reason for his visit. He knew from the file he'd studied that the boy was ten and the girl was nine.

"That's Karim and Laila," Angela confirmed over his shoulder.

"Nice names."

"It was difficult finding names which we both liked and were suitable for our mixed English and Saudi cultures so when I was pregnant the first time, we made a list of possible names, which were acceptable to both of us. We agreed if it was a boy, he could choose any name off the list and if it was a girl the same thing applied for me. He chose Karim and next time around I chose Laila."

Powell took the cup of milky coffee he'd requested and sat in a very soft armchair while Angela sat on the striped sofa.

"I hope Brian has informed you that this is an introductory meeting. I haven't yet decided whether to help you," Powell explained. Then seeing the look of anguish on her face he quickly added, "It's not that I don't want to help you, it's just that I don't want to take your money under false pretences and give you hope without any chance of success."

Angela regained her composure. "That's very honest of you Mr. Powell but frankly you are my last hope and I'd pay you anything you ask, even if there was only a one per cent chance of success."

"Please just call me Powell." He took a small notebook from his pocket. "Why don't you start at the beginning and tell me about how you met your husband?"

"We met at the dinner party of a mutual friend. I've always been attracted to foreign men. I'm not very keen on the typically emotionally stilted English types."

Powell looked up from his notebook and raised his eyebrows.

"Sorry," she apologised. "But I grew up in a family where to show emotion was shocking and by my twenties, I realised I wanted something different in a man to what I was expected to be dating."

"Had you ever had a relationship with anyone else from the Middle East?"

"No, Baz was my first. I'd been out with mostly Latin types before Baz. You know, French, Italian, Spanish." She smiled, then added, "I did a lot of travelling in my twenties. Of course, my friends warned me against marrying an Arab. Unfortunately, I don't tend to listen to other people once I've set my mind on something. Pig headed, my mother used to call me."

Powell had to hold back a smile. Angela was turning out to be a little different to what he'd expected and he knew he was quickly being sucked in by her personality. It was soon going to be very difficult, if not impossible, to refuse to help.

"What did Baz do for a living when you met him?"

"He worked at the Saudi embassy as some sort of cultural attaché, helping people to get visas, work permits, that sort of thing. Pretty boring job but he always said he really enjoyed living in England. I can't actually imagine him living in Saudi."

"I understand Baz comes from quite a wealthy family?"

"That's true but I didn't need his money. I'm a wealthy woman in my own right. I'm an only child and I inherited more than I can ever spend when my parents died."

"What did his parents think of their son marrying you?"

"Baz admitted they didn't approve but they were always polite to me and they loved their grandchildren. I didn't actually see them very much. They came over only rarely and Baz took the kids over there once or twice a year."

"I assume your husband didn't just wake up one day and decide he no longer wanted to live with you? Had you been having problems in your marriage?"

"You know, the usual thing, we just drifted apart. It turned out we had little in common. He spent too much time working and when he wasn't working he was playing golf. I felt like a single parent at times."

"There was no one else involved?"

"Not really."

"What does not really actually mean?" Powell probed.

"I had a one night stand with someone and it brought it home to me that I was too young to continue in a loveless marriage. Baz and I hadn't had sex for months and I suspected he might be having an affair but I had no proof. In fact, the only evidence was that he stopped wanting to have sex with me so I told him I wanted a divorce. He simply said it was impossible."

Powell was surprised by her frankness. "So what happened next?"

"Nothing much really. Baz was a little more considerate and I just had second thoughts, thinking it would be the best for the kids if we tried and stayed together. Three months later he took the kids to see his parents as usual after Ramadan and that was the last time I saw them." A tear formed at the corner of her eye, which she wiped away with her hand. "Sorry. That was almost twelve months ago."

"Don't apologise. As a parent, I think what he's done is unforgivable." Powell still thought of himself as a parent despite Bella's death. He wondered if that was odd?

"They went for ten days and he called me the day before they were due back, announced he'd done what I requested and obtained a divorce. In Saudi Arabia it's very easy for a man to obtain a divorce. Under Sharia law a man has only to say 'I divorce you' three times and he is divorced."

"Can a woman do the same?"

Angela laughed. "You have a lot to learn about Saudi Arabia. It is almost impossible for a woman to get a divorce unless the husband agrees."

"What happened next?"

"He told me as Laila was over seven and Karim over nine, he had been given custody and I wouldn't see them again. Can you believe that once a boy reaches nine and a girl seven, the mother has no parental rights? Under Islamic law the woman's job is finished!"

"How old are they exactly?"

"Karim is ten and Laila is just nine."

"It sounds like he had been planning it ever since you mentioned wanting a divorce."

"That's what I believe. I wish I'd gone about things differently. I was very naïve but Baz always seemed so western in his attitudes. I never dreamt for a moment he could do such a thing."

"Where were you married?"

"Dubai."

"Why Dubai?"

"It was like many things in our marriage, a compromise. I am a non-practising Christian. Baz could not marry me in anything resembling a Christian ceremony. If his family were to attend as he wanted, they would not approve of alcohol or men and women mixing. And don't mention dancing! So he suggested Dubai because it's a short distance from Saudi and they are far more laid back. So we had the full on traditional Muslim wedding but then his family went back to Saudi and next day I had a second celebration with my family, with plenty of drinking and dancing!"

"I didn't realise a Muslim could marry a Christian."

"A Muslim man can marry a Christian woman but not the other way around. If you want my opinion, the Muslim religion is basically designed to give men the opportunity to do whatever they want and women just have to toe the line and God, or perhaps I should say Allah, help them if they ever question anything. Do you know women aren't allowed to travel, work or study without the permission of a male relative? I couldn't even drive a car by myself the one time when I visited Baz's parents."

Powell drank some of his coffee to gather his thoughts. "I've been doing a little checking and it seems Saudi law says what Baz has done is perfectly legal."

"So my solicitor informs me and it seems the court order I have, ordering him to return the children, isn't worth the paper it's written on. I've become quite an expert on these matters. There's no extradition treaty between us and Saudi Arabia, and they haven't signed up to the Hague Convention concerning child abduction so I have basically hit a brick wall. That's why

Brian suggested you may be able to help."

"How do you know Brian, by the way?"

"Our families have always been friends."

"Brian discreetly checked with the Saudi embassy and was informed Baz simply requested to return home, which given his length of service in the UK was deemed a perfectly reasonable request. They pointed out he had done nothing wrong."

"Nothing wrong for a Saudi man maybe."

"By the way, do the children speak much Arabic?"

"Much better than me. Baz always spoke to them in Arabic from when they were very young so they aren't quite fluent but it's pretty good."

"Angela, I really would like to help but what you are asking may be impossible."

"I realise I am asking a great deal and you would be putting your life in danger but I don't know where else to turn. I thought of visiting Saudi and confronting Baz's parents but it turns out it's virtually impossible for a woman in my position to obtain a visa. I spoke with the Saudi Embassy and they weren't very helpful. I would need a male family member or someone else in Saudi to sponsor me and that isn't going to happen. Even if I could get to Saudi, it's impossible for me to move around the country freely so I would have almost no chance of being successful. It's driving me mad being stuck here unable to do anything."

Angela sounded desperate and Powell believed if he refused to help she would indeed try something foolish by herself, which was surely doomed to failure and could see her end up rotting in a Saudi jail. It was something which wouldn't sit easily on his conscience.

"This has to be planned meticulously," he explained. "I will need access to significant funds…"

Angela interrupted him by jumping out of the sofa, rushing to him and wrapping her arms around him. "Thank you so much. You don't know what this means to me."

Powell held her silently in his arms for a minute as all her pent up emotion poured out in tears.

"Our chances of succeeding are not good," he said, gently pushing her away and looking her straight in the eyes. "All I can do is promise that I will do everything in my power to bring your children home."

"That's all I can ask. Brian told me you were the best man for the job"

"What else did Brian tell you about me?"

"He said you would be cautious about taking the job but I shouldn't worry. You would definitely agree to help in the end."

CHAPTER SEVEN

When Powell returned to the bar, Afina was keen to hear how his meeting had gone.

"So, are you going to help this woman?" she immediately asked before he even had time to take off his jacket.

"Yes I am."

"I knew you would. You are a good man."

Powell had to smile. Afina seemed to have a very high opinion of him, which wasn't one he always shared. He had simply been unable to refuse Angela Bennett's desperate and emotional cry for help. He knew he wouldn't be able to handle the guilt of refusing to help and reading in the newspaper she was in a Saudi jail or worse.

On a practical level it would keep him busy for the next few weeks and stop him dwelling on recent events. He was scared of finding himself with too much free time on his hands because he knew that would be when he would dwell on what had happened to Bella. It had been that way when her mother died and it was a dedication to learning kickboxing which had enabled his to return to some form of normality.

He knew if Bella had still been alive, he wouldn't have contemplated something so risky as helping Angela Bennett because he would have hated the thought of something happening to him and leaving Bella on her own. Since her mother died, he had felt an additional responsibility for her upbringing as her sole parent.

Bella's death left him with no one to think about but himself. That wasn't really a healthy way to live your life. He needed something to give a damn about and he'd been touched by Angela's story. Even though he couldn't see Bella again, he could try and ensure Angela did get to see her children.

"I expect you to look after the bar while I am gone," Powell stated.

"I should come with you," Afina suggested. "I can help."

"And who would run my bar? I need someone here I can trust."

"You can trust me."

"I know I can. Anyway, you couldn't come to Saudi. It's a very strict

Muslim society. As a woman you could do nothing alone and if we travel together we would risk being charged with immoral behaviour and thrown in jail."

"Are you serious?"

Powell simply nodded his head in response.

"My God! I had no idea," Afina responded, evidently shocked. "If I can help in any way without actually visiting the country you must let me know. If you need any research or anything?"

"Don't worry, I will be sure to ask for help when I need it."

"Please promise to take care," she pleaded. "I don't feel ready yet to inherit this bar." Afina was referring to the fact he had made her the sole beneficiary in his will.

"I plan to live to a hundred. Everything will be fine and I shall be back before you've had time to miss me." Powell decided to change the subject. "Have you spoken with Mara? How is she doing?" Mara had spent several weeks in hospital recovering from a serious gunshot wound received while saving Afina's life. She had been in a coma and not certain to recover at first but the prognosis now was she would fully recover.

"Bored and wanting to leave hospital but the doctors say she must stay a little bit longer," Afina replied. "She is definitely much better because I have seen her flirting with the nurses. Both the male and female ones!"

"That sounds like Mara. Where will she go when she leaves hospital?"

"She is thinking of going back to Romania to recuperate but she plans to come back to Brighton when she is completely recovered."

"I assume you have told her about Dimitry?"

"Yes, in her words, she will not be shedding any tears for the bastard."

Powell's phone rang and he wasn't surprised Brian hadn't wasted any time finding out how his meeting with Angela had gone.

"Hi Brian."

"I hear from Angela you've agreed to help."

It was the first time Powell had heard Brian refer to Angela rather than Mrs Bennett and an uncomfortable thought crossed his mind. Could he have been the one night stand Angela mentioned?

"I'll do whatever I can to help," Powell confirmed. "But it isn't going to be easy. In fact, it's very nearly bloody impossible."

"Good man. Listen, I should warn you that in the event of anything going wrong you'll get zero help from our government. We do a huge amount of business with the Saudis. Even more importantly, Saudi are considered vital partners in the fight against terrorism and ISIS in particular. It's not a boat we ever want to rock."

"I understand that but there are a few things you can help with."

"Why am I not surprised to hear that!"

CHAPTER EIGHT

Powell had arranged to meet Brian for lunch at the same Thai restaurant in Belgravia, where they had rekindled their friendship a few weeks previously, after not having been in touch for nearly twenty years. Powell had given a great deal of thought as to how to confirm where in Saudi the children were living and he was hoping Brian could point him in the direction of some much needed specialist expertise.

Powell entered the restaurant to find Brian already seated at a table.

"Good to see you, Powell," he said, shaking hands. "Glad you're in one piece. You must tell me all about Bucharest."

"To be honest, I hope I've seen the back of the place," Powell replied, as he took his seat.

The waiter arrived before Powell could add anything further. They ordered a bottle of dry white wine and some water.

Powell gave a detailed account of his time in Bucharest while they studied the menu. The wine was delivered and their orders for food taken.

"To Dimitry," Brian toasted. "May he rot in hell."

Powell tasted the wine and nodded approvingly. "That's good and probably not cheap."

"Meal is on me today. The least you deserve after what you've been through."

"Thanks, Brian. You know, it's difficult to believe Dimitry was part of the same human race as the rest of us."

"I know what you mean but sadly there are far too many Dimitry types around the world. Trafficking is now as lucrative as the drug trade."

"Are the authorities doing enough?"

"They've been slow to respond but I think they are improving, albeit slowly."

"Listen, can I ask you to check on Adriana when you have a chance? They have done the right thing and hidden her away somewhere safe but now they won't let Afina speak with her and she's getting worried. As you can imagine, Afina's a bit paranoid. She thinks the police are all corrupt. Can you just check she is okay?"

"I'll do my best. How is Afina otherwise?" Brian asked.

"Making me more and more superfluous at the bar. She catches on quick and works hard."

"And does she still have a crush on you?"

"Maybe a bit but I'm sure it will soon wear off."

"And what are your feelings for her?"

"For god's sake, Brian, I didn't come here to be interrogated."

"Sorry. You know, rock stars and actors go out with much younger girls all the time."

"But I'm neither and she deserves better."

"I can't argue with that," Brian laughed.

"Thanks for nothing."

Powell drank some more of his wine, then said, "Let's talk about Saudi."

"Not sure I could live out there," Brian stated. "I'm too fond of a glass of wine."

"I could just about skip the wine but beer's another matter."

"Well I assume as you suggested taking me to lunch, you need my help with something? Hopefully not something that will cost me my job," Brian said, good naturedly.

"Twenty years ago, when there wasn't such a thing as the internet, I would have gone out there and searched for the kids by knocking on doors. That worked okay in the past but in Saudi, I suspect would just draw attention to myself and not necessarily be fruitful. The kids are probably registered as living somewhere or at least attending a particular school. I need someone who is capable of hacking into Saudi public records and finding me answers."

Brian took a large drink of wine. "It's not something I can help with officially."

"And unofficially?"

"I might be able to point you to someone who can help. We do have our own internal teams but we also sometimes use outside experts when we need to have deniability. I don't know them personally but I can ask around and get a name for you."

"That would be a great help. If I can get some hard information about where the kids are living before I go out there, then I can start trying to formulate a plan for getting them out."

"Just give me a couple of days."

"There's one other immediate way you can possibly help. I need a visa for Saudi and from what I've been reading it seems there is no such thing as a tourist visa for non-Muslims. So I'm thinking a business visa which allows me multiple visits over six months would be best and I thought you might be able to help with the cover story?"

"I'll arrange everything. Probably find a friendly bank where you work and you're visiting local Saudi branches for meetings. The banks have become very amenable to these types of requests since the government dug them out of the shit."

"Sounds good. I might have some other requests but that's it for now."

"So let's enjoy lunch, forget about the bad guys for a bit and discuss the state of the English cricket team."

CHAPTER NINE

Powell arrived early at the address on the outskirts of Maidenhead, having allowed himself plenty of time to get around the M25 but for once there had been no traffic problems. He found himself outside a large detached home, which wasn't what he'd been expecting. For some reason, he'd thought to find a small dingy office with a geek huddled over computers but this was a very middle class home in an affluent part of town.

He knocked on the door and was further surprised to find it answered by a young, attractive girl in her twenties.

"I'm here to see Samurai," he said, feeling slightly foolish and worried he may be at entirely the wrong address.

"He's out back in the office."

Powell relaxed and followed the girl through the house to the kitchen.

"I'm Tina by the way. Would you like something to drink? Tea or coffee maybe?"

"Powell," he replied and shook hands. "Coffee would be good. White, no sugar, please."

"I'll bring it out to you. Peter's down there," she said, pointing out the window to a large log cabin at the bottom of the garden. She emphasised his name as if the idea of him being called Samurai was absurd. "He's expecting you."

Powell followed the path to the cabin and opened the door to find Samurai facing him, sat behind a large desk with two giant monitors and surrounded by an assortment of computers and printers on smaller desks. Samurai was very tall, skinny and looked even younger than the girl indoors. Powell couldn't imagine anyone looking less like a Samurai. Perhaps that was the point of the choice of name.

"I'm Powell," he said, extending his hand.

"Sorry, I don't shake hands with strangers. Too many germs."

Powell was a bit taken aback and dropped his hand to his side. "No problem." Looking around the office he could see it was clean if full of technology.

"I was told you needed my help and it's a good cause," Samurai said, coming straight to the point.

"I need to locate two children who have been abducted and taken to Saudi Arabia by their father."

"Anything I can do to bash the Saudis is good with me."

"You don't like Saudi Arabia?"

"Are you serious? After what they've done to Raif Badawi."

"Sorry, I'm not familiar with him."

"The Saudis have thrown him in prison for ten years and sentenced him to receive one thousand lashes for promoting freedom of speech on his blog. I can't believe you haven't heard of him."

"I've been kind of busy in other directions recently," Powell apologised with something he thought was a bit of an understatement. He'd thought about nothing except Romanians for far too long.

"So what do you need me to do?"

"I can give you the names of the children and their father. I want you to find out where they are living. I have the grandparents address where they may be staying. I'd also like to know if they are going to a local school."

"Shouldn't be too hard to check. I might need some help because of the language but I know someone who does speak Arabic and I think he'd love to help."

"How long will it take?"

"If it's urgent I charge two thousand pounds a day and can start tomorrow. Otherwise it's one thousand pounds a day and I'll fit it in as and when I can over the next month."

"And how many days will it take?" Powell queried, shocked by the daily rate.

"Probably no more than two or three but you can never be sure. I'll check in with you at the end of each day with a progress report and you can decide whether or not I continue."

Powell knew he had no other options. He now understood how this couple in their twenties were living in such a grand house.

"It's important you don't leave a trail," he stressed. "If this father knows we are looking for the kids he is quite likely to spirit them away."

"Is this man important?" Samurai asked suspiciously. "I mean is he part of the Royal family or something?"

"No, nothing like that. He met the children's mother while working here at the embassy and his family are wealthy so he probably has a few contacts in the right places."

"Is he some form of spook?"

"No, he doled out passports and work visas."

"Good, only I don't need some bleeding fatwa against my name."

"This is everything you should need," Powell said, placing the small USB Flash Drive containing all the information he thought Samurai would need, on the table.

Samurai took a wipe from a packet on his desk and gingerly cleaned the USB drive, careful not to allow the drive to come into contact with his skin. Satisfied with his cleaning, he then pushed the drive into his computer.

"Thanks. I'll be in touch tomorrow." Samurai stated, looking up and seemingly surprised to see Powell was still present.

Powell turned as the door behind him opened and Tina entered with two cups of coffee.

"He's just leaving," Samurai said rather dismissively as Powell took hold of his mug.

It seemed, no matter the rate you paid, you shouldn't expect too much pampering. Samurai was just as much an oddball as Powell had originally expected.

"Come drink it in the house then," Tina suggested.

"Bye," Powell said but Samurai ignored him and was already staring intently at his screens.

"Sorry if Peter was a bit rude," Tina said, once back in the kitchen. "He's very focused on his work"

"Glad to hear it, given the rates he charges."

"His social skills could be a bit better," Tina smiled.

"I don't mind as long as he gets the job done."

"He's very good at what he does. There's always more work than he has time."

"Have you been together long?"

Tina laughed and pulled a strange face. "We've been together a very long time but we aren't a couple! Peter is my younger brother."

CHAPTER TEN

Powell had spent the two weeks before his trip conducting further research into Saudi Arabia in general and Riyadh the capital in particular. When he discovered the holy month of Ramadan, when Muslims fast during daylight hours and seek to purify their soul, was not due to finish for another few days, he had delayed his journey, not wanting to add further complications to his visit.

Samurai had delivered the important news that the children did indeed seem to be living with their grandparents in Riyadh. They were attending a nearby school and the address given on the application was that of the grandparents' house.

The difficulty was not going to be initially taking the children but how to get them out of the country. The Saudis had stringent visa and exit controls, which meant it wasn't going to be a simple case of flashing UK passports and getting on the first available plane. After further discussions with Brian and speaking with some expatriates on online forums, there appeared to be four possible exit strategies though none were immediately appealing and all carried severe risks.

The first possible exit was by plane and use bribery to get through airport controls. Corruption was common at border crossings but Powell also knew that half the people who took your money never delivered on their promise.

The second possible exit was via the King Fahd Causeway linking Saudi with Bahrain. Every weekend enormous numbers of people would make the short drive across the causeway to enjoy the night life, drink and prostitutes of Bahrain. Again though it would still be necessary to bribe someone on the Saudi side of the frontier.

The third possibility was to drive across the desert to a neighbouring country and avoid all immigration controls. The last option was to take a boat from a Saudi port or somewhere along the coastline and again avoid legal checks.

Powell felt unable to make any decision as to the best exit strategy until he was in Saudi and able to better evaluate the different options. In fact, whichever option he chose, he was also going to have at least one if not two backup plans. He would be thorough in his planning and fortunately Angela Bennett was a wealthy woman, able to fund a variety of alterative options.

Brian had come through with the business visa, which allowed him to make multiple visits over the next six months, although no one visit could be for more than thirty days, which suited his purpose perfectly.

Powell travelled business class on British Airways from Heathrow and enjoyed a couple of beers, knowing they would be his last until he returned in a week's time. As the pilot announced they were getting close to their destination, he watched as several sophisticated women in elegant western fashions went into the toilets and came out in black abayas covering their whole body. The complete transformation of the women served as a reminder of the cultural differences between where he was coming from and where he was going.

The plane landed at King Khalid International Airport, which was the most imposing and architecturally amazing airport Powell had ever used, evidence of the country's wealth. The plane stopped at a stand and he joined the queues for immigration. The inside of the airport was air conditioned to the extent of almost being cold.

As he emerged without any problem from the customs hall into arrivals, he was descended on by taxi drivers fighting for his fare. He agreed a price with one driver based on what his research told him was the correct amount to pay for the trip into the city centre. Leaving the air conditioned comfort of the Terminal for the first time, he was assaulted by the fiercest heat he had ever known. Even the short walk to the taxi left him sweating profusely and feeling drained.

The taxi took him to the Sheraton hotel, located close to the financial district where he supposedly was visiting a major bank for business meetings. For the first time in his life, he was staying in a luxury hotel and had an unlimited expense account, which was a far cry from his days working for MI5, when hiding away in run down dumps was more the norm. Then again, Belfast didn't have much in common with Riyadh.

For this trip, he had decided the best way of remaining unobtrusive was by joining the many business travellers, who typically would stay in a very smart hotel and gorge on the five star food and shopping, when not working.

He was impressed with his large hotel room and modern furnishings. There was even a mini bar but without alcohol. The room service menu looked good, which suited him as he didn't plan to sit eating alone in restaurants. He'd been told that you could get some of the best fish dishes you could find anywhere in the world and as he loved fish he was looking forward to putting his information to the test.

The hotel had a gym, which Powell planned to use each day. He had been putting in extra training at his kickboxing gym, not so much because he expected to meet any trouble on this reconnoitring trip but more because he was concerned about being fully effective in the crushing heat, he anticipated and had now experienced. He had read that with an arid, desert climate, Saudi is nearly always baking hot but is at its worst in July. He would need to stay fit and hydrated if he was to operate at maximum effectiveness.

Thanks to the Internet, Powell had already located Baz's family home and was familiar with all the streets in the vicinity. He was unsure about moving around on foot as he suspected a European would attract too much attention but how busy were the streets? The whole point of this trip was to answer such questions. He would hire a car in the morning and investigate.

Powell had a file of information on his laptop, which was protected by a complex password. Nothing on his person disclosed his real reason for visiting Riyadh. He ordered ribeye steak and chips from room service, despite his penchant for fish and reread everything in the file. Confident he was as prepared as he could be, he turned out the lights and set his alarm for an early start.

CHAPTER ELEVEN

Powell hired a BMW Z4 from the desk in the hotel's lobby. It was the same as he drove at home, which he reasoned should minimise the learning curve of driving on the wrong side of the road. The one change was the addition of air conditioning, which wasn't needed in Brighton but was essential in Saudi. While the car was delivered to the hotel, he stuffed himself on a huge breakfast buffet and read a local English language newspaper.

Once sat behind the wheel of his shiny new BMW, he wondered if he had made the right choice. On the one hand there was a familiarity to the inside of the car but everything was in the wrong place! If he had hired a completely different car he wouldn't have had any expectations about where to find the instruments.

He set the Sat Nav system to the address of Baz's parents and headed down King Abdullah Road. The traffic was quite busy and more than once his left hand moved towards an imaginary gear stick before he remembered it was now on his right. Fifteen minutes driving and a few turnings later, he found himself at his destination. He drove straight past the large home surrounded by a high, brick wall, which ensured the privacy of the occupants. A little further down the street he made a turning and found space to pull in at the kerb.

The road on which the house stood had a collection of large properties down both sides of the street. It was very much a residential area with no shops and he was going to stick out like the proverbial sore thumb if he went for a walk.

The task he'd set himself seemed so daunting he was tempted to drive away and forget the mad idea of rescuing Angela Bennett's kids. Instead, he drove around the block and took in the surroundings. Next, he drove past what he thought was the school the children attended but again everything was hidden behind a large brick wall and there was none of the usual noise you would expect to hear from the playground of an English school around lunchtime. Then he remembered it was July and the schools were closed for holidays just like in England.

After a few further minutes driving around, Powell lost his bearings and found himself emerging on to King Fahd Road, opposite advertising for a shopping mall, describing itself as the largest in the Middle East. He wondered if it was somewhere Baz and his family might visit. It was certainly very close to where they lived.

He decided to visit the mall, which was called Al Mamlaka and take a look around. The mall was located in a huge skyscraper and once he'd parked, he found himself in a shopping centre like nothing he'd ever experienced before. The building had impressive air conditioning, which offered a great respite from the oppressive heat on the streets.

Full of stylish designer names and beautiful shop fronts, in his mind it seemed more suited to California than the Middle East. Then again, the Saudis had to spend their oil wealth somewhere. Everything was sparkling clean and ultra-modern with huge ceilings.

He walked around and looked in a few shops but wasn't in Saudi to go shopping so it was only idle curiosity, which made him go inside. He noticed that unlike in England, there wasn't a single female shop assistant in any of the shops.

There were plans of the different floors and one floor was described as being for women customers only, so they could shop in privacy and comfort, which made him smile. Presumably it would be staffed by female shop assistants, which would be useful in the stores selling lingerie and other female orientated products.

The mall was so vast it didn't seem overly crowded, certainly not like the shopping centre back home in Brighton, which was minute in size by comparison. Never having been a great fan of shopping he knew it wasn't a place he would visit often if he was a local.

He found a Starbucks on the ground floor, ordered a Latte and sat watching a mixture of locals in their long white thobes and foreigners in suits walking past.

Having finished his coffee, he browsed in a few more shops, then discovered that from the mall there was access to the Four Seasons hotel, which was equally grand. He decided this would be where he would stay if he was to return. It was close to Baz's parents' house and would make a good base. He decided he'd seen enough for the time being so headed back to his hotel.

He was learning that he had to be alert with his driving. The Saudis were quite happy to cut him up at excessive speeds and turn into his road with little thought for his presence. It seemed once Saudi men were behind the wheel of a car, they became excessively macho and drove without thought for any other driver.

CHAPTER TWELVE

Powell spent a couple more days driving around Riyadh, familiarising himself with the neighbourhood nearby where the kids were living and also the major road connections to the airport and other locations, which might be needed for backup plans.

He was grateful for the air conditioning as the temperature outside was forty two degrees and he was spending a great deal of time in his car. The heat made it practically impossible to move around on foot for anyone except a local. As a result, he had not spotted a single other European on the streets around where the children were living and knew he must stay in his car or risk drawing unwanted attention to himself.

He didn't know much about Baz but he had executed the very smooth abduction of his children and was no fool. If he heard of a fair skinned foreigner hanging around his neighbourhood, he might very well put two and two together and realise what Powell's presence meant.

He was also having to be mindful of prayer times because whenever the call to prayer came around, shops would all shut up pretty quickly ten or so minutes before and he felt he became even more conspicuous. He had discovered that Muslims turned to Mecca and prayed five times every day so he had taken to asking at the hotel reception for prayer times each day before going out.

On the third day of his visit and in order to maintain the pretence of the reason for his visit, he had lunch with a senior banker called Martin Thwaite. He turned up at the bank's offices in a smart suit and his arrival was recorded, should anyone wish to check in the future.

Thwaite was friendly and seemed completely unfazed by the lie he was perpetrating. He had chosen a very smart restaurant, no doubt guilt free about the cost as he thought he was helping his government.

After food was ordered, Thwaite spent five minutes describing the supposed purpose for their meeting and what they had discussed in case Powell was ever questioned.

"Now that's out of the way is there anything I can help you with during your stay?" Thwaite asked.

"You can tell me a little about life in Saudi. What would you tell an employee about to relocate here?"

"If you're married don't bring your wife."

"Why is that?"

"They get bored. There is only so much shopping and sunbathing you can do. Life becomes very repetitive and mostly lived in the compound. My wife quickly became frustrated with the lack of freedom. If you have young children then I suppose you have less time to fill but we can't have kids."

Powell found it impossible not to immediately think of Bella whenever children were mentioned. "How long are you here for?" he asked, wanting to change the subject.

"Fortunately our two years is up in a couple of months. Our next posting is Singapore, which will be very different and frankly, we can't wait. If I'd had to do another year here, I think I would have been facing a divorce."

"If I stayed here for any length of time, I know I'd miss having a beer, especially given this climate."

"You can get beer if you want and most other things but only within the confines of the compound or the embassy. I believe they bring bottles into the country inside the diplomatic bags. Personally, I don't think it's worth the risk of being discovered by the Mutaween so I keep well away from alcohol. It's been good for my weight, I've lost over a stone since I've been out here."

"Who are the Mutaween?"

"The religious police. Their job is to enforce Sharia law. They have virtually unlimited power and can arrest you just for talking to a woman who is not your close relative."

"Doesn't sound like much fun."

"It's okay as long as you keep to their rules. I have a demanding job, which keeps me busy. I think it's harder for an expatriate wife who can't work and has too much time on her hands. Tessa isn't really one for too many coffee mornings and sitting around doing nothing by the pool all day."

"So why do so many people come here to work?"

"The tax free salaries. If you're sensible, and it's difficult not to be here, then you should be able to save significantly more than you ever could back home."

"I understand many people drive over to Bahrain for the weekend."

"They do. In fact, we've done it a few times ourselves. It's particularly appealing to single men looking to let their hair down. There's a host of clubs, bars and any form of entertainment you want. It's also relatively cheap so on a Thursday night the causeway looks like the M25 on a very bad day."

"Can you tell me a bit more about the whole process of visiting Bahrain? What are the controls like at the Saudi border?"

Thwaite raised his eyebrows and placed his cutlery back down. He leaned forward and spoke quieter. "The checks are thorough but if you have money, as with everything in this country, then anything is possible."

CHAPTER THIRTEEN

On the fifth day of his visit, Powell finally hit the jackpot. He was driving down the by now familiar street where the house stood and suddenly the large double doors swung open and a smart, black Range Rover pulled out into the traffic just in front of him. The car had tinted windows so it was impossible to see who was inside but with a surge of excitement he slowed his speed, while at the same time keeping a clear view of the car up ahead.

Within a couple of minutes they were back on King Abdullah Road, then they quickly turned right along Takhassusi Street. Five minutes later the car up ahead parked outside a brightly lit shop called The Marble Slab Creamery. Powell slowed down as he passed and could see that despite the slightly confusing name, the shop was in fact an ice cream parlour.

He pulled to a halt a little further down the street and quickly jumped out of the car and started walking back towards the parlour. Up ahead he could see two excited children rush from the back seat of the car and head inside the parlour. It was strangely exhilarating to see the children in person at last. They were the whole reason for his being in Saudi.

At a slower pace an elderly woman, who had been sitting in the front passenger seat followed the children into the parlour. He guessed she was probably their grandmother although in her black robe it was impossible to be certain and she could have been a servant just as easily as the grandmother. She wasn't wearing a burqa so her face was visible and he could determine she was elderly. The driver stayed hidden behind the tinted windows.

Powell was pleased to see the children looked well. In fact, they looked very happy and not like two children missing their mother very much. Then again it had been a year and he had no idea what they had been told by their father. A small part of him wanted to grab the children there and then but he knew he wouldn't get far kidnapping them off the street, with no plan to exit the country.

He wondered what he would do if the children were so happy with their father they didn't want to go back to England. It wasn't something he had previously considered. He wasn't going to be able to drag them back screaming and kicking. It was something he would have to give careful thought to, in his planning.

Powell stood in line behind the grandmother as the children chose toppings for their tubs of ice cream. He heard the kids speak Arabic with the person behind the counter and also with the grandmother. There was considerable laughter and discussion about which toppings to choose. Both children seemed highly proficient in Arabic and they had quickly adapted to their new way of life.

As the grandmother left the parlour, he could see out the corner of his eye, she gave him a quick look of appraisal but he was busy studying the different types of ice cream laid out behind the counter so all she saw was the rear of his head.

Powell ordered a tub of cookies and cream by pointing at what he wanted, then walked slowly back to his car. He didn't need to follow the Range Rover any further, he had the confirmation he needed. Next time he met the children it would be under very different circumstances.

CHAPTER FOURTEEN

Back in England, Powell arranged to meet again with Angela Bennett and give her an update on his trip.

"The children looked well," Powell added, having recounted the details of the trip to the ice cream parlour.

Angela had been hanging on his every word. "I can't believe you've actually seen them. And they looked happy?" she asked doubtfully.

"They were getting ice creams. All kids love ice cream."

"True. I guess I should be happy they are happy. It's just, I suppose a little part of me has been imagining them desperately unhappy and missing me."

"I'm sure they are missing you but children adapt to new circumstances very easily."

Angela was thoughtful for a second, then composed herself and asked with renewed spirit, "So what are you going to do next?"

"I plan to go back in about two weeks' time. I expect to then spend a further couple of weeks in preparation and sometime in my third week, all being well, I will bring the children home."

"What's your plan?"

"It's still early in the planning stage and please don't take exception to this but I would rather not share any details of my plans with anyone."

"But these are my children. I want to know what you are planning to do. I don't want them put in danger."

"I promise to look after your children like they are my own. I won't intentionally put them in any danger. And if I don't succeed, there is no reason to expect their father to hold the children responsible for my actions. Any retribution he wants will be aimed solely at the two of us. So I won't share any details of exactly what I am doing or when with anyone until it is absolutely necessary. You have to trust me."

"I do trust you. Brian says you were once the best undercover operative in MI5 but he wouldn't tell me why you left the service at such a relatively young age. He said I should ask you."

"My wife was killed as a result of my work. I left to bring up my daughter."

"I'm so sorry."

"Someone pointed her killers towards me and let them know where to find me. Whether it was intentional or just a careless conversation someone overheard in a pub, I don't know. But if you want me to proceed to the next stage these are my non-negotiable terms, I will only share with you what I consider is necessary to achieving my plan. If I seem paranoid I'm sorry but it's not without reason."

"I think I told you the first time I met you, I would be willing to pay anything and do anything to recover my children. You are my only hope so I will abide by your rules, even if I don't like them."

"Thank you. So what I can tell you is that in about five weeks, I need you potentially available at very short notice to travel just about anywhere to meet your kids."

"So you're not planning to bring them straight back to England?"

"That is still to be determined but I want you available to see your kids the moment I get them out of Saudi. They'll be feeling lost and vulnerable and will need to see you to know everything is going to be okay."

"Believe me, in order to see my children again, I will be available to fly anywhere at a moment's notice."

"I know, I just wanted you to be prepared."

"Powell, do you think I am being selfish trying to bring them back to England. If they are happy where they are, then maybe they would be best left with Baz?"

"It's my view that young children are best with their mothers."

"But you have brought your daughter up by yourself."

"Out of necessity but I firmly believe Vanessa would have done a better job. Not that I was a bad father, just I know how much Bella missed not having a mother at certain times."

"I understand that Bella being a girl, would miss not having her mother around during puberty and many other times but I have a daughter and a son. Wouldn't a boy similarly miss having his father around?"

"Possibly but I'm no expert. What I do know is that you gave birth to both children and it's Baz who has selfishly chosen to abduct your children. He made no attempt to come to some amicable arrangement about seeing them. From what you've told me, he didn't spend a great deal of time with them when he lived with them, he spent more time working and playing golf. Now it suits him, he's behaved terribly. So I don't think you're being selfish wanting to bring them home. I'm not convinced anyone who acted as Baz did can really claim to be the right role model for children."

"Thank you. I needed to hear some encouraging words. My life has become very lonely over the last year."

"Keep your spirits up"

"I will. How is your daughter by the way? How old is she now?"

Powell hadn't wanted to volunteer the information but couldn't avoid answering. "She died a few weeks ago. She was a police officer and murdered doing her job."

Angela was visibly shocked. "I had no idea. Brian should have told me. Here I am going on about my children but at least they are alive. I'm so sorry."

"Actually, working on recovering your children is the best possible form of therapy. It's helping me to deal with my loss."

"I can't believe I was lucky enough to find you. You're a very special man, Powell."

"Let's focus on your children, not me," Powell said gently.

Angela got up from the sofa and walked towards a mahogany drinks cabinet. "I need a sherry. Would you like one?"

"Better not, I'm driving."

Angela poured a large measure of sherry into a wine glass, tasted it and then sat back down. "There could be another problem I hadn't really thought about until now. What if they don't want to come with you? They seem happy with their father and you're a stranger. I always taught them to be wary of strangers."

"I've thought about that and I don't have all the answers yet but I will be prepared for that possibility when the time comes."

"I wish I could come with you."

"That just isn't possible. Do you have something special that belongs to you or the children, which will prove I am working for you and help them go with me."

Angela was thoughtful for a minute then answered, "I need to think about what would be best."

CHAPTER FIFTEEN

Powell had asked Brian for a recommendation and been given two names. Neither man was personally known to Brian but he had asked internally for suggestions and been told both men were very reliable contractors. Powell had invited the one he deemed had the most relevant experience to Brighton for the day.

Both men had impressive CVs but the man called Jenkins had done fifteen years in the Paras with several tours of duty in Afghanistan and Iraq, before leaving the army with the rank of Staff Sergeant, to spend three years in Oman working for the Royal family. The additional Middle East experience made him Powell's first choice.

Powell had Afina ask him if he wanted something to drink and then brought him to the office.

"I'm Powell," he said, rising from behind his desk. He shook hands and found his hand held in a vice like grip.

"Jenkins," the man replied in a Welsh accent, looking him straight in the eyes before finally letting go of Powell's hand. He was about six feet tall with a muscular body but it was his red hair and freckles, which immediately caught Powell's attention. The CV had already revealed he was thirty nine years old.

"Take a chair," Powell beckoned. Jenkins had been stood to attention like he was on parade and it made Powell feel a little uncomfortable.

Jenkins did as instructed and still managed to maintain a ramrod straight back, even when sitting.

Jenkins came straight to the point. "I understand you have an urgent job you need my help with."

"I do and you come highly recommended."

"Pleased to hear it."

A knock on the door was followed by Afina entering with two coffees. She placed them on the table and quickly left.

Powell took a sip and then explained, "Two children have been abducted by their father and taken to live in Saudi Arabia. I'm going to bring them back home to their mother."

Jenkins had his cup halfway to his mouth and paused to take in what he'd heard. "That isn't going to be easy," he said with conviction, before taking a sip of his coffee. "But it does sound like a worthwhile operation."

"It's very worthwhile. Our client hasn't seen her children for twelve months and there are no legal avenues available to help her but you're right, it isn't going to be easy. In fact, it will be extremely difficult and dangerous. If we get caught, the best we can hope for is to spend at least twenty years in a Saudi Jail for kidnapping, although I have to be honest with you and say the penalty could be death."

"Certainly make a change from the normal jobs I get given," Jenkins responded, smiling for the first time. "We'll have to try hard not to get caught."

"So are you available for the next six weeks?"

"The timing's good. We should be finished just in time for the world cup."

"A rugby fan?"

"I'm Welsh aren't I?"

"When's the England versus Wales match?"

"End of September."

"Our visas will run out mid-September so we'll definitely be back in time."

"I need a couple of days to tie up loose ends then I'm all yours."

"Great. I have a contract for you to sign. The pay is one thousand pounds per day plus expenses. There will also be a payment of one hundred thousand pounds paid to your next of kin in the event of your death. In the event of ending up in any jail, all legal fees will be covered."

"Sounds more than fair. Where do I sign?"

Powell pushed the contract across the table and handed Jenkins a pen, who signed and returned the contract without reading any of the small print.

"Now that's out of the way, let me give you some more background, then we can grab some lunch."

CHAPTER SIXTEEN

Powell had spent a considerable amount of time discussing every aspect of the operation with Jenkins but the big outstanding question of exactly when and where they would grab the children, could only be resolved once they were in Saudi. Powell appreciated Jenkins' eye for detail and it was a great help to have someone to bounce ideas off. He also had a dry sense of humour, which often had Powell in stitches. Within a few days of working together, Powell was sure he'd made the right choice for the operation.

Powell had timed his return trip to Riyadh, to coincide with the children returning to school in a week's time, which he reasoned would give them another possible scenario for taking the children. It would certainly mean the children following a routine and routine enabled the formation of a plan. At least that was the theory.

Powell had emphasised to Jenkins that their final plan could not include any action which might result in any deaths. While that applied especially to the children's family, he was also determined no innocent locals should be harmed during their operation. If they were caught and had been responsible for anyone's death, it would seal their own fate, as it would become inevitable they would receive the death penalty for their actions.

Although it wasn't just for selfish reasons Powell didn't want to see anyone killed. He was no longer the gung-ho agent of twenty years ago. With maturity he had learned to value all lives as important, including the locals in Saudi Arabia. It could not be success at any cost. That was the approach of people like Dimitry.

For two days, Powell had showed Jenkins the routes around Riyadh connecting the house with the school, ice cream parlour, shopping mall and airport. Powell made Jenkins drive so he became familiar with the unique Saudi approach to driving, which was based on not giving a damn for anyone else on the roads.

By the third day, they both decided they were fed up of driving everywhere and needed some exercise. Operationally, they also felt they needed to expose themselves to the extreme temperatures, to understand the effect on their bodies, should they end up on foot at any time. A run was out of the question but they decided to take a walk and the weather dictated they should make an early start to the day so they could be back in their hotel, before the worst of the suffocating heat arrived.

They left the hotel at eight and despite a slower than normal pace were soon suffering from the stifling heat.

"All the time I spent in Oman, I was never stupid enough to go for a walk just for the hell of it!" Jenkins exclaimed after walking for half an hour.

"Only time I've experienced heat like this was in Greece but I was laying by a pool with a beer in my hand," Powell replied with a grin. "Let's head back. I think we've learned everything we need to know about the climate. Basically, if we end up running for our lives on foot we're as good as dead."

"You should have warned me you were such a cheerful optimist before I took the job."

"What's going on here?" Powell asked, noticing a large group of people gathered in the square up ahead.

"Let's take a look. I could do with some distraction."

They had a wall of people in front of them blocking their view from whatever was capturing the attention of so many people.

"Perhaps it's their equivalent of Covent Garden," Powell suggested. "You know, where you get the amateur jugglers and comedians performing."

As they came near to the group they could hear the voice of a woman screaming in Arabic and obviously distressed.

"What the fuck!" Jenkins swore, once having a view of what was transpiring.

A couple of locals at the back turned around in surprise but quickly returned their gaze to the events being played out in front of them.

Powell's eyes were drawn to the scene of a police car parked in the centre of the square and the half a dozen khaki clad policemen standing in a semi-circle. What had caused Jenkins outburst, was the sight of a woman covered in white from head to toe being held by two of the policemen, obviously protesting her innocence as the police men pushed her to the ground. A few other men in typical Arabic clothes were stood around.

A tall man dressed also in white, was talking to one of the men in uniform and two of the other men. When he turned away from his conversation, there was an audible intake of breath as the large curved sword he was holding came into view. The sun glinted on the metal as he raised the sword high in the air.

The woman was all the time screaming but now it was evident she wasn't just protesting her innocence but begging for her life. Powell looked at Jenkins for the first time, who appeared equally shocked.

The executioner shouted at the woman on the ground and she knelt without moving but all the time she was still shouting and begging. He brought down his sword to the edge of her neck but then stopped. It was obviously a trial swing to prepare his aim. One look from the executioner towards the man in Arabic dress he had just been talking with, was met by a nod of assent. His sword came down in a whirl of speed and the woman's screaming was halted for all time.

Her head fell to the ground, rapidly followed by a stream of blood spurting from her body, which after a few seconds fell sideways to the ground. Men hurried forward with a stretcher to recover the body.

"Let's go," Powell urged.

The crowd were already starting to disperse and their presence had caught the attention of some of the locals. Powell knew that since the beginning of time, public executions had attracted crowds but he couldn't understand why so many people would want to watch such a spectacle. Was there really so little to do in Saudi that an execution passed for entertainment?

"I've never seen anything so barbaric in my life," Jenkins said, as they hurried away from the square.

"I wonder what the hell she did to deserve to die like that?" Powell asked.

"No woman deserves that. I don't care what she's done," Jenkins replied, shaking his head in disbelief. "I've seen some things as a soldier but I've never seen anything like that before and I hope I never have to again. It's a good thing this country is alcohol free as otherwise I would be getting very smashed today."

"I must admit I could do with a proper drink. I'm going to call my banker friend. He says you can get anything you want if you know where to go."

CHAPTER SEVENTEEN

Powell and Jenkins were in the living room of the villa belonging to Martin Thwaite, which was part of a large compound of homes hiding behind a solid brick wall, isolating the real Riyadh from the foreigners living inside the compound. The Saudis needed the expertise of the foreigners but didn't want the expatriates contaminating their morals.

"Thanks for the invite," Powell said. "After what we saw earlier today, we both felt like a stiff drink but common sense has now prevailed and we'll be happy just with something cold."

"How about some champagne?" Thwaite asked.

"Are you serious?" Powell queried suspiciously.

"Saudi champagne. Tessa serves the best in Riyadh," he said, smiling at his wife.

"I'll give it a try," Powell agreed.

"Me too," Jenkins concurred.

"Just be a minute," Tessa said and left for the kitchen.

"Why did you need the drink so badly if you don't mind my asking?" Thwaite inquired.

"We saw a woman beheaded in public in the centre of Riyadh this morning," Powell answered.

"Ah! You had a taste of Saudi justice at first hand."

"I wouldn't call that justice," Jenkins expressed. "No matter what she'd done."

"Actually the case has been in the news. She was accused by her husband of killing his brother."

"Did she do it?" Powell asked.

"She claims her husband killed his brother in an argument then blamed her for his death."

"What was the evidence?"

"The husband swore it was her and that was sufficient evidence."

"But wasn't it just his word against hers?" Jenkins queried.

"Yes but his word is worth ten times hers because he is a man."

"You have to be joking?" Powell said.

"Sadly not," Tessa affirmed, returning from the kitchen with a tray of drinks. "Women just don't count in this country. They are simply men's chattels."

"I think I'm learning that." Powell said. "Are there many of these executions?"

"There were about eighty I think last year," Thwaite answered. "A large number of them were beheadings in Deera Square or as foreigners like to call it - Chop Chop Square."

Tessa handed out the glasses of champagne.

"That's not bad," Powell said after tasting. "What's in it?"

"It's essentially fizzy apple juice with some fresh apple, orange and mint added plus an extra squeeze of lemon so it doesn't become too sweet."

"Quite refreshing," Jenkins said. "But I've never been much of a one for even real champagne. I'm more of a beer man myself."

"So what are you two doing in Saudi?" Tessa asked.

"Just some boring business meetings," Powell answered.

"Do you work for the bank?"

"No, we're consultants," Powell answered.

"Let's not talk work," Thwaite suggested.

"Of course not," Tessa agreed.

The doorbell chimed and Tessa announced, "That will be Lara."

"I didn't know you'd invited her," Thwaite said with a hint of annoyance.

"You couldn't expect me to spend the evening alone with you three men, talking work all night?"

As Tessa walked to the front door, Thwaite shrugged his shoulders at Powell. "I asked her not to invite anyone else but despite living in Saudi, I'm afraid the local ways haven't rubbed off. She doesn't like being told what to do."

Powell smiled. "No problem."

Tessa quickly returned, accompanied by a strikingly attractive, slim woman with olive skin and a huge smile. She had long dark hair and Powell guessed she was in her early thirties.

Introductions were made and they all went through to the extended kitchen where the dining table was located.

"What do you do in Saudi, Lara?" Powell asked once they were seated.

"I teach English at the International school."

"She does a bit more than that," Tessa added. "She is the deputy Principal."

"Where are you from originally?" Powell asked.

"I was born in London. My father is Lebanese and my mother English so I speak both Arabic and English. My father is a Christian though, not a Muslim."

"And how do you come to be teaching in Saudi?"

"To be honest, I had been through a messy divorce and felt like I needed a change. I applied for the job on a whim and was a bit surprised when I was offered the position. I think my ability to speak Arabic was probably what swung it in my favour."

Powell was always impressed by anyone who could speak more than one language. Somewhere in his distant past, he had gained an O Level in French but learned at a young age his smattering of vocabulary wasn't much help when actually visiting France. There was something very alluring about the combination of Lara's beauty and her heritage.

"How long have you been living here?" Jenkins asked.

"Twelve months and I've another two years left on my contract."

"Are you enjoying it?" Powell inquired, realising he had been staring a little too hard. She had an unnerving way of looking at him, as if she could read his thoughts. He hoped to hell she couldn't.

"It's like any job, there are good and bad bits. I like the tax free money, the life here in the compound and I get the chance to use my Arabic. I've never been a big drinker so don't miss the alcohol. If I close my eyes to what goes on around me, it's a good life."

"You missed our visitors telling us about their morning experience at Chop Chop Square," Tessa said.

"Did you see that poor woman executed?" Lara quizzed.

"Barbaric it was," Jenkins replied.

"Not by design," Powell explained. "We stumbled upon it while out for a walk."

"You went for a walk?"

"We wanted some fresh air and went early to miss the worst of the sun."

Lara had a slightly disbelieving expression. "So why are you two visiting Saudi?"

"Bank business," Powell replied.

"You don't seem like the normal banker types," Lara stated.

"You're right we're not. We're actually consultants working for the bank, doing risk and security assessments."

"I promised the guys we wouldn't talk about work," Thwaite intervened. "They aren't actually supposed to talk about what they do. It's all highly sensitive so let's change the subject."

"That type of consultant," Lara said knowingly. "How long are you planning to stay here?"

"About three weeks," Powell replied. "Perhaps you can recommend some things we can see while we are here?"

"There are some interesting sites if you get some time off. I hear the edge of the world is worth a visit but I've never been."

"We have," Tessa said. "It's a long drive, about two hours, but worth it for the amazing views."

"How about something closer to home?" Powell asked.

"Being a single woman here means I don't really get to visit many places. I'm sure Tessa could suggest things."

"There's a fort and a museum, which are just about worth a visit." Tessa suggested.

"I don't want to be a heathen," Jenkins interjected. "But I'll give all this tourist stuff a miss if you don't mind. I'm not really interested in visiting anywhere. After this morning's experience, I think I'll spend my free time by the hotel pool."

"If you want a change, you can always come over here again. A night of bowling and fast food is fun if you get fed up of all the fancy food at your hotel!" Tessa suggested.

"That does sound like fun," Powell agreed. "Perhaps Lara can join us again?"

"I'd like that," Lara replied. "It's interesting meeting new people and this compound is very relaxed so I don't have to cover up and men and women are allowed to mix freely."

Powell liked the idea of seeing Lara again and not just because she was an attractive and interesting woman. He thought she might be able to help with their plans. "The compound is very impressive," he said.

"It's one of the best in Riyadh," Thwaite replied. "Only westerners are allowed to live here."

"As jails go, I suppose it isn't bad," Tessa moaned. "The house is nice and there's a good pool."

Thwaite said nothing verbally but his look suggested it was a subject which had been debated many times in their household.

"Security seemed pretty good at the gate," Jenkins mentioned.

"It's recently been stepped up because of threats made by ISIS," Thwaite replied. "And the targets aren't just us foreigners. Saudi pilots fly alongside the Americans and Brits bombing ISIS in Iraq. I think the terrorists are doubly offended by a Muslim country working alongside the Americans. Make no mistake, ISIS have their eyes set firmly on Saudi and their wealth. They want to start an insurrection."

"Well it's lucky then we won't be here much longer," Tessa said.

"Enough talk of terrorism," Lara begged. "It's putting me off my dinner!"

CHAPTER EIGHTEEN

Powell and Jenkins spent the next ten days becoming completely familiar with the children's routine. At six forty each morning on Sunday to Thursday, they were driven to the school gates. At three thirty the car was parked outside the school to collect them and they returned directly to the house, not to leave again for the rest of the day.

On the Friday, Powell had his first view of Baz as he and the kids took a trip to the nearby shopping mall. They did some shopping and had some lunch in a café. Powell and Jenkins kept their distance but it appeared the children were happy enough.

On the Saturday evening, the children visited the same ice cream parlour where Powell had followed them on his previous trip to Riyadh. The routine of the visit was as before, with the grandmother taking the children inside while the driver remained outside.

Powell welcomed the strict routine of the children as it provided the opportunity for reasonable certainty in their planning. Each evening he and Jenkins spent ages discussing the pros and cons of the different possible locations to snatch the children. They had to plan for all eventualities including the children not wanting to go with them. They were prepared to use some force to carry the children away if necessary but it would only be as a last resort.

Powell decided they deserved a break and arranged through Thwaite that they should all have an evening of bowling and burgers at the compound. In truth, he was wanting to see Lara again more than he wanted to bowl. Over a few pints in a pub back home, Jenkins would be decent enough company but as a regular dinner companion, the conversation was definitely running dry.

Powell was impressed with everything about the compound and the presence of serious looking guards as they arrived, conveyed the impression you were crossing the border into something akin to the Vatican in the heart of Rome. This enclave though was a retreat from the religious society outside rather than the other way around.

They met at Thwaite's house and then walked to the bowling alley, which was probably less than half the size of those back home. Everyone professed to rarely going bowling, which in Powell's case was definitely true.

"How about a little wager to make it more interesting?" Thwaite suggested. "Us three locals against you two. We take our average game score versus your average. Losers pay for dinner."

"Is that fair?" Jenkins asked. "I mean you'll have two women on your team. We'll have an unfair advantage."

Powell had to bite his lower lip to stop himself howling with laughter when he saw the look on the faces of both Lara and Tessa."

"Only joking," Jenkins smiled with a wink. "I love winding up the girls."

Powell had suspected the compound inhabitants may have been playing down their ability. After three frames in which the opposition had all scored a mixture of strikes and spares, he knew who would be paying for dinner.

"You're all pretty good," Powell observed.

"Not much else to do of an evening," Tessa smiled.

"This is fun," Lara said. "I don't get to mix with many single men." Then she quickly added, "Not that I'm like desperate for a man or anything. It's just everyone on the compound bar two of us are married."

"Do you go home for holidays?" Powell asked.

"I've been a couple of times."

"I understand quite a few people like to visit Bahrain at the weekend."

"I went once with a girlfriend but it's not really my cup of tea. The place was full of men getting drunk and Chinese whores."

"Does that include Saudi men or was it just expatriates?

"It's a mixture. Young Saudi men are bored with their lives. You can see them hanging around the shopping centres just trying to get a glimpse of the women going shopping. Most of the malls now don't allow single men inside. It's a messed up society."

"Then why do you stay?"

"It's good tax free money. In two years I hope to save enough to buy a house when I return."

"I was reading how many people have problems with leaving the country. Employers don't keep the paperwork up-to-date and visas expire etcetera."

"The school is very good about these things, although I did know someone who wasn't allowed to leave because he was accused of having debts. The company where he worked went bust and he was held responsible despite he didn't own the business or anything, he was just a salesman."

"What happened to him?"

"A friend at the embassy knew someone who could help him leave unofficially. Some money passed hands and he made it out through Jeddah airport before he was thrown in jail."

"Tessa tells me you have been to a few parties at the Embassy."

"Yes, I've been to quite a few. They are quite fun and that's where I met the salesman. I get an invite because most of the staff have kids at my school."

"How do you get around for an event like that as you're not allowed to drive or go anywhere with a man?"

"I use a taxi company especially designated to take women. I used to sometimes go shopping with Keith, the man I was just telling you about. If anyone had asked we would simply have said we were married but we were never questioned."

"Every day I spend here I learn something new. Perhaps you can answer something else I've been thinking about which is, why do all the women wear black?"

"Out of fear of attracting the attention of the religious police. If they all wear black then nobody stands out. The women here are all terrified of being accused of any impropriety."

"The woman we saw beheaded was wearing white."

"When a woman is executed or dies she wears white."

"Whenever I hear you speak about how women are treated in this country you sound disapproving but you choose to work here."

"It's not a perfect world. Surely you have learned that by now. Even in the UK women have only had the right to vote for less than one hundred years. At least the women here have enough food and clean water."

"Speaking of food, I don't know about you but I'm hungry so I better take everyone's orders as it seems I'll be paying."

"I'll have the Texan burger with fries and a coke, please."

"Be right up. By the way, what was the name of that guy at the embassy with the contact, just in case I ever need some help."

"Barry Daniels. If you do ever need him, mention me. I think he has a bit of a soft spot for me."

CHAPTER NINETEEN

Afina arrived a quarter of an hour later than usual at the hospital to visit Mara. She had developed a routine of working the lunch shift at the bar then spending about ninety minutes with Mara before returning for the night shift. Afina considered Mara her best friend and would eternally be grateful to her for saving her life.

Today Afina was delayed by her bus simply not turning up, which had now happened a few times. She needed to learn how to drive. When Powell returned she would ask him for some lessons but she doubted he would let her learn in his smart BMW. Afina was wondering if she should buy a small car when she walked through the double doors, which led to the hospital ward where Mara was one of twelve patients recovering from serious operations.

Afina pulled up quickly when she spotted the man sat at Mara's bedside. She instinctively turned and retraced her steps. Safely on the other side of the doors, she realised she was breathing fast and experiencing something akin to a panic attack. She hadn't recognised the man but every man she had ever met, who was associated with Mara, had been the epitome of evil.

Afina stood wondering what to do next. She could simply walk away and come back tomorrow to see Mara. What was she thinking? Mara was her friend and she might need her help. Mara had selflessly thrown herself in the way of a bullet to save Afina and almost been killed. She felt ashamed of her cowardice.

Afina walked purposefully back through the doors and up to Mara's bed. The man turned towards her at the sound of her footsteps and the smile on Mara's face announcing her arrival.

"Hello Mara. How are you today?" Afina asked in English, which she wouldn't normally do when visiting. She turned towards the man and held out her hand. "Hello, I am Sorina," she lied. Some self-preservation instinct told her not to use her real name.

"Gheorghe, I am Mara's uncle," he replied in English with a thick accent.

"Pleased to meet you," Afina responded, trying hard to remain calm. Mara had told her about her gangster uncle. It was he that had taken Mara's virginity and made her into a prostitute. Afina had already decided that anyone who could treat their sister's child in such a way, was the lowest of the low.

"Are you Romanian?" he asked.

"Yes I am."

"How do you know Mara?" he queried, switching to Romanian.

"I met her in the bar where I work."

Gheorghe appraised Afina from top to bottom. "You are a very pretty girl. I would have no problem finding you more interesting work."

"Uncle, Sorina is a very good friend of mine and knows what I do for work but she does not approve so we do not talk about it."

"She could earn far more money than working in a bar."

"I enjoy my work," Afina replied, indignant. "Money does not buy happiness."

Gheorghe turned back towards Mara. "When do the doctors say you can leave? We need you back at work as soon as possible."

"Are you mad," Afina interjected angrily. "Mara can't work for a very long time. She almost died."

"I was not speaking to you," Gheorghe replied dismissively.

Afina couldn't believe Mara's uncle could be so callous. "You should go back to Romania. You are not welcome here."

Gheorghe jumped up from his chair and raised his arm as if to strike her. "You should watch your mouth," he warned.

"What's going on here?" a nurse asked, scuttling to the bedside. "You have to leave," she instructed Gheorghe.

"I will leave when I want to," he responded. "I have not finished."

"Leave now or I will call security," the nurse warned not at all intimidated.

"I will see you again," Gheorghe threatened, turning to Afina and giving her a menacing look as he gave up the argument and walked away.

"Are you all right? the nurse asked Mara.

"Fine thanks. I apologise for my uncle, he is from Romania and not an easy man."

"Most men aren't in my experience but in here he will behave himself or we won't let him come again."

"I'll tell him," Mara said with a smile.

"Good." The nurse seemed satisfied and left with a reassuring smile.

"What was he doing here?" Afina asked, sitting in the chair vacated by Gheorghe.

"He is looking for Danny but doesn't know his real name is Powell. I'm so happy you said your name was Sorina, which suits you by the way, because he also asked if I knew where to find you."

"I don't like your uncle."

"I don't know anyone who likes him but people are afraid of him. Back home he is an important man. People do not answer him back like you did. You need to keep away from him because he will not forget what you have done."

"Is he here alone?"

"I doubt it, he never goes anywhere without at least a couple of bodyguards. He is visiting Stefan tomorrow."

"Are you worried about something Stefan will tell him?"

"No, believe it or not Stefan has always stuck up for me against his father. He will say nothing that makes things worse for me."

"Stefan is strange. I can't say I like him but he is different to the others like Dimitry and Victor. He is less of an animal."

"If you had been brought up by my uncle you might have turned out very different. Stefan had no choice about his life."

"Enough talk of Stefan. Do the doctors still say you can leave next week?"

"Yes, as long as there are no new complications."

"I assume you are no longer planning to go home?"

"You heard my uncle, he wants me to stay here."

"Then you must come and live with me," Afina encouraged. She had been trying to convince Mara for a couple of weeks not to go home but to no avail. She wanted to look after her friend and start to repay her for what she had done. Now, thanks to her beast of an uncle maybe it was possible.

"And lead my uncle straight to Powell? I don't think that is a very good idea. You must warn Powell about my uncle."

"He is working abroad at the moment so I will wait until he returns."

"You should not wait. You don't know my uncle. He is extremely dangerous."

"I will tell him soon. So where are you going to stay. Surely not with your uncle?"

"Emma and Becky have offered to let me stay with them and I am going to accept, at least for a short time."

Afina saw the sense in Mara's staying with their mutual friends. All three were also lovers. "That is a good idea," Afina conceded. "But no wild sex parties, you are not yet fit."

"You sound like my mother," Mara laughed. "Actually, it's funny you mention sex because I masturbated yesterday for the first time since I was shot. I think I must truly be getting better."

"Mara!"

"If you want to help me recover even quicker you could slide your hand under the blankets and…"

"Can we please change the subject?" Afina interrupted.

"I like teasing you," Mara admitted, with a broad grin.

"Let's be serious for a moment. What are we going to do about your uncle?"

CHAPTER TWENTY

Powell and Jenkins followed the children and their father to a different shopping mall from the previous week, a bit further from where they lived. The change of shopping centre was the first variation in routine they had observed in over two weeks of studying their movements. Powell was pleased by the change in location as it added weight to their choice of plan.

The last couple of weeks had taught them everything they needed to know about the children's routine. They had decided they would snatch the children the following Saturday at the ice cream parlour. They would then go direct to the airport where the contact provided by Barry Daniels at the Embassy, would meet them and guide them through the passport controls on to a British Airways flight to Heathrow.

The timings worked well as the visits to the ice cream parlour normally took place around six in the evening. It would take ten minutes to drive to a nearby taxi rank, where they intended to leave the BMW and grab a taxi to the airport. The BA flight left at just after midnight so they had about five hours to spend at the airport when they would be exposed to the risk of the Saudi police searching for them.

They had come up with a plan to persuade Baz his children were being kidnapped for financial reward and he would be instructed not to involve the police if he wanted to see his children alive again. As they couldn't speak Arabic, they had prepared a note which they planned to leave on the car windscreen with the instructions. They would be calling the next morning to discuss the handover of the money except by then, they hoped to be safely in England. They were asking for one million Saudi Riyals, which converts to roughly one hundred and seventy thousand pounds. It wasn't perfect but it was the best solution they could come up with.

The children and their father had followed the same pattern as the previous week, doing some shopping and then taking coffee and cakes in a café. Powell and Jenkins were sat far enough away not to be noticed but in a position where they could see the family.

"So it's definite?" Jenkins asked. "Next Saturday we snatch them at the ice cream parlour."

"Yes. It isn't exactly fool proof but it's the best we can manage. I just hope this Muhammad guy can be trusted."

"He's charging enough money."

"What the fuck was that?" Powell asked.

"That's gunfire," Jenkins replied, rising from his seat. There was the sound of two explosions. "And unless I'm much mistaken that's grenades."

People around them were standing, unsure what to do or what was taking place.

"It's coming from the floor below," Powell confirmed. He looked around and could see Baz leading his children away from the café. "Let's stay with the children."

Screams could be heard mixed in with the gunfire. People began running away from the café in random directions as further people were emerging from the escalator screaming and obviously panicked. Acrid smoke was also drifting up the escalator.

Baz was leading the children towards the escalator going up to the next floor. Strangely he seemed the only one heading upwards and then Powell remembered it was the floor for women where men were not allowed.

Powell was first off the escalator at the top and was confronted by the sight of Baz arguing with two armed guards. They were pointing their guns at Baz and the message seemed to be a very clear go away.

Seeing Powell and Jenkins the guards started shouting something in Arabic in their direction.

"We don't speak Arabic," Powell explained. "There are terrorists downstairs shooting people."

Again the guard shouted something in Arabic. Behind the guards, Powel could see women hanging around in groups, many of them on their mobiles.

"The fool says we are not allowed here," Baz said, turning to Powell and speaking English.

The sounds of gunfire were becoming louder and more frequent.

"Sorry but we don't have time to discuss this any further," Powell said. He looked at Jenkins and nodded. In the same instant, he took the extended arm of the guard nearest and twisted it behind his back, forcing him to drop the gun. As the second guard turned towards Powell, Jenkins similarly disarmed the man.

The guard was babbling on nonstop in Arabic so Powell forced his arm a little higher up his back and he understood to be quiet.

Powell shoved the guard to the floor and quickly stepping away, he recovered the gun, which had earlier fallen from his hand. He pointed the weapon at both guards, which allowed Jenkins to release his hold on the other guard and collect the second weapon from the ground. Jenkins put his hand on the shoulder of the guard still standing to make him understand he should join his colleague sitting on the floor.

Women were starting to scream as they saw what Powell had done.

"Don't worry, we're the good guys," Powell shouted. Then turning to Baz he said, "Can you please tell them we're on their side."

Baz shouted out something in Arabic and the screaming subsided.

"Tell everyone to move to the far corner," Powell instructed. "Away from the escalator."

A man started to run up the escalator but fell backwards as he was shot in the back. Powell swiftly turned and shot the terrorist responsible. He kept his eyes fixed on the bottom of the escalator, in case other terrorists would come to the aid of their shot friend but no one appeared. It was undoubtedly chaotic down below.

"Let's move now," Powell shouted towards the women, seeing they all seemed frozen to the spot.

Baz again translated into Arabic and bellowed at the women in a voice that demanded they obey. The screaming returned but the women did move quickly away from the escalator.

There was a floor plan by the side of the escalator. Powell studied it and could identify two other ways to access the floor, the lifts and the stairs, which were both situated close together at the opposite end of the floor to where he was directing the women to go. He assumed there would be further armed guards stationed by the lifts and stairs but Powell had already observed the guards weren't very effective. They were not frontline police just shopping mall guards, who had probably never seen action.

Powell motioned with his weapon for the guards to get to their feet. They both stared at him suspiciously. Jenkins hauled one up by his collar and the other stood up as well.

Turning again to Baz, Powell said, "Tell the guards to get on their radios and find out what is happening. Is help on its way?"

Baz translated and one of the guards spoke into his radio.

After a moment the guard put down his radio and said in decent English, "The security forces are on their way."

"Go with the women and try to keep them calm," Powell ordered. "Build some form of defensive shield if possible while we try to buy time until the cavalry arrives."

The guard said something in Arabic to Baz.

"Speak bloody English," Powell barked.

"Sir, I cannot go with the women. Many of them are single. It is not permitted."

"This is an emergency," Powell stressed.

"He is right," Baz agreed. "We cannot take the risk. We might avoid the terrorists but this is not England, it is too great a risk."

Powell shook his head, finding it unbelievable the men should be more scared of the consequences of mixing with the women, than the terrorists who were trying to blow their brains out.

"Then I suggest you guards go see what has happened to your colleagues and see if you can help them. Don't let any terrorists onto this floor."

The guards seemed eager to get away and ran towards the lifts.

"What can I do to help?" Baz asked.

"Take your children into that shop," Powell sugegsted, pointing to the nearest designer clothes outlet. "Find somewhere to hide the kids and make sure they keep quiet and don't come out, no matter what they hear."

Baz hurried away and Powell turned to Jenkins. "We can cover the escalator from here but keep an eye out for anyone coming from the lifts. I doubt the local guards will last long in a fight."

There seemed to have been a lull in the gunfire but then the quiet was broken by a large explosion.

"That wasn't just a grenade," Jenkins stated.

"We sure could do with finding out what's going on down there," Powell replied. "Hold the fort here for a minute. I'm going to go take a look."

Powell pressed the emergency red button at the top of the escalator and as expected it stopped moving. He inched his way down the steps, keeping low. From about hallway down he could see what was happening on the floor.

About five gunmen were watching over a large group of about thirty shoppers who had been grouped together and sat on the floor. Every so often another gunman would herd further people into the group. They were rounding up all the shoppers, either to kill them or act as hostages. Powell hoped it was the latter reason.

At the bottom of the escalator he could see the terrorist he'd shot. There were grenades attached to his belt and what looked like an AK47 beside his body. He sat on the escalator so he wasn't visible to the gunmen and slid down the stairs to the bottom. He reached forward and dragged the gun back without anyone noticing. He didn't want to push his luck so didn't try for the grenades. He moved back up the escalator and took another look.

He didn't understand why the gunmen hadn't yet tried to access the third floor. Was it because they knew only women shopped on the floor and they were after the men? Or were they just being careful and clearing the building one floor at a time? He had seen enough and crept back up to join Jenkins.

"They're rounding up all the shoppers," Powell explained. "This might come in useful," he said, handing the AK47 to Jenkins, who with his army background would have more experience with such weapons.

Jenkins inspected the weapon. "This is the real deal, not one of those cheap imitations." He put the pistol in his waistband. "How many of them did you see?" Jenkins queried.

"I counted seven but there may well be more."

They were both crouched at the top of the escalator, one either side.

"Sounds like the troops have arrived," Jenkins stated, as there was a sudden increase in gunfire and explosions from the ground floor.

"I have a bad feeling about this," Powell voiced. "Those hostages have little chance if the Saudi security forces arrive all guns blazing."

They both turned and raised their weapons at the sound of approaching footsteps.

"I can't just hide like a woman," Baz said, crouching beside them.

"Your security forces have arrived," Powell explained. The sounds of gunfire were now continuous. "The terrorists have rounded up all of the shoppers on the floor beneath us. It could turn into a bloodbath if the security forces don't try and negotiate."

"Can we help the hostages?" Baz asked.

"It's probably not the smart thing to do," Powell answered but knew he would not be able to sit by and ignore the terrorists shooting the hostages.

"I understand," Baz said. "Can I borrow your weapon and I will try to help the hostages."

"You must think of your children," Powell replied. "And we have a duty to protect all the unarmed women on this floor."

"This man can stay and protect the women," Baz said, indicating Jenkins.

"Ever fired a gun?" Powell asked.

"Yes."

"Give him the pistol," Powell said to Jenkins.

Jenkins handed the gun over and Baz took it confidently. Powell could immediately tell Baz was familiar with handling guns and wondered where he'd gained the experience.

"If we hear shooting below, we'll use the escalator for cover and move down the stairs to see if we can help," Powell said. "Don't do anything foolish," he warned.

Powell had no time to add any further instructions. The sound of rapid fire and shouting on the floor below was quickly followed by a series of deafening explosions and flashes of light.

Powell moved down the escalator but at the bottom could see little. There was thick smoke and chaos punctured by automatic weapons fire. He reckoned the explosions had been a mixture of stun grenades and smoke grenades because two of the terrorists nearest to him were looking very disorientated.

As he raised his own weapon, both terrorists fell to the ground shot by men in uniform emerging from the smoke, wearing masks. Powell ducked back down out of site.

"They have it under control," Powell said to Baz. "Let's get out of here."

He started to move back up the escalator but Baz seemed intent on remaining.

"I suggest you follow me, if you don't want to be mistaken for a terrorist wielding a gun."

Baz seemed to suddenly understand the implication of Powell's words and quickly followed him back to the top.

The shooting had diminished to just an occasional shot. Powell wondered if that was the security services not wanting prisoners and making sure the terrorists were all dead.

"What do we do next?" Jenkins asked.

"We put the weapons down and wait."

CHAPTER TWENTY ONE

Powell and Jenkins had been ushered out the building to safety with no questions asked. For once, Powell realised, it was an advantage to be an expatriate in Saudi. The security services never considered for a second they were anything other than unlucky foreigners caught up in the attack.

They had placed the weapons out of sight behind the counter of the shop where they were waiting with the children to be rescued. Baz had seemed to understand it was the best way to avoid potentially awkward questions. He wanted to get the children home as soon as possible. Powell had been very tempted to take one of the weapons with him but he couldn't risk being searched as they left the building.

At some point in the future, the security guards they had disarmed would tell their story and the female witnesses would speak of the two Europeans, who had dared to encroach on the women only floor of the building. They might even speak in positive terms but Powell hoped they would simply forget all about them, otherwise there would be too many questions to answer.

An investigation may commence or equally it could be decided there really was nothing worth investigating, given the more urgent need to track down any remaining terrorists. Either way, there was nothing further Powell or Jenkins could do to hide the truth. They had wiped the guns free of prints but their faces might well be on CCTV. If someone was intent on searching hard enough for them, then they could be found but Powell hoped they would be out of the country before they were identified.

Safely outside on the street, Baz had formally introduced himself and the children. He then asked Powell to watch the children for a moment while he went and spoke with a police officer. Now the adrenaline had subsided, Powell was finding the situation rather surreal. He was in Saudi to break up this seemingly happy family and had a gnawing doubt about his operation. Baz had certainly been a concerned father, worried for the safety of his children.

Powell had an interesting tale to tell Angela Bennett. It was possible that if they hadn't been there to gain access to the floor, the guards would have made Baz and the children return downstairs, where they could easily have been killed. In a roundabout way, Angela Bennett may well have saved her children's lives.

"You speak very good English," Powell said to the children.

"We were born in England," Laila answered. "We used to live in Kingston."

"How long have you been living in Saudi Arabia?"

"Since our mother died," Karim answered. "About a year ago."

Powell was taken aback by the response. "I'm sorry," he said simply, casting a glance at Jenkins. Now wasn't the time for revealing their mother was very much alive. "Do you like it here?"

"I prefer England," Laila answered quickly.

Karim shot his sister a glance of disapproval. "It's different to England but I like it here. This is a better place for a Muslim to live."

Powell decided to say nothing further as he didn't want to cause a rift between the children.

They were surrounded by literally hundreds of others who had also been evacuated from the building. Smoke was billowing from one particular part of the building and glass from broken windows littered the pavement.

Ambulances were everywhere, sirens wailing and ferrying the injured to hospital. There were people being treated for a wide variety of injuries. The walking wounded were almost being ignored as the medical staff prioritised the most urgent cases first and loaded them in the back of the ambulances. Many of the people looked dazed and in a state of shock.

It was a scene of utter confusion and for a second Powell wondered about just leaving the children and getting as far away as possible. He was becoming increasingly uncomfortable the longer Baz spent talking to the police. What if he was already telling them about the two Europeans, who had attacked and disarmed the guards? After what seemed an eternity, Baz finally turned and walked back alone.

"We were very lucky," Baz said. "I'm told the terrorists shot many of the hostages. There may be as many as fifty dead."

"Why are Muslims killing Muslims?" Jenkins asked. "I don't understand."

"It is the price we pay for supporting the Americans and fighting terrorism," Baz explained. "We live in difficult times."

"We do indeed," Powell agreed. "And the worst thing is I can see no end to the problems."

"I share your pessimism," Baz agreed. "But now I need to get the children home. Thank you both for your help. I would be honoured if you would have dinner with me sometime soon."

"It would be our pleasure," Powell agreed, despite feeling a little uncomfortable at the idea. It could only benefit the operation to find out more about where they lived.

"Good, this is my number," Baz said handing over a business card. "Call me tomorrow and we can arrange something. Where are you staying by the way?"

"The Four Seasons."

"That is very close to where I live. It is also where I normally take the children shopping. I chose a bad day for a change in shopping mall!"

"All's well that ends well."

"Ah yes, one of your many good English sayings. Give me a call, my cook is excellent and will prepare a feast for us to celebrate our survival."

"I'll call tomorrow and we can arrange something," Powell confirmed.

"Now I must try to find a taxi," Baz said. "I fear it may be several days before I can reclaim my car from the car park."

Powell and Jenkins watched the family walk away and then hurried away in the opposite direction.

CHAPTER TWENTY TWO

Afina was working in the bar. It was a midweek lunchtime so mostly busy with local office workers and mothers out shopping. She was planning to finish a little early as Mara had left hospital a couple of hours earlier and Afina was keen to go visit her, Emma and Becky.

She was working behind the bar, which she mixed with sometimes clearing tables and serving food. The best thing about the job was chatting to the customers and getting to know a few of the regulars. It was hard work but since her days as a gymnast, she had never been afraid of hard work.

Her heart missed a beat when she saw Gheorghe and two others enter the bar and sit at a table. They picked up the menus and by the time they glanced around the bar, she had already turned around and walked to the office.

Why were they here? It surely couldn't just be a coincidence they had walked into this bar out of the hundreds in Brighton and Hove. She doubted they knew this was where she worked. Gheorghe probably hadn't given her another thought since they met in the hospital, which meant they were here because they knew it was owned by Powell. Whether they also knew Powell and Danny were the same man was still uncertain.

Afina peeked out the office and catching the attention of one of the servers, waved him over.

"Luke, I know those three men at table eight," Afina explained. "And I don't want them to know I work here. When you serve them can you please tell me anything they say? And remember you've never heard my name."

"Of course, Afina. I'll go take their orders and let you know."

It was possible that Gheorghe was here to check out Powell because he would know it was him who killed Victor. He would also know it was Dimitry who murdered Powell's daughter. Would Gheorghe be looking for revenge for Victor's death? If they were good friends it was a distinct possibility.

Luke went from taking the orders to the till where he entered the details.

Then he returned to the office.

"They asked about Powell," Luke said. "I told them he was out of the country and they asked when he was due back. I said I had no idea but didn't think it was for a couple of weeks."

"Thank you, Luke. They didn't mention me?"

"No, they only seemed interested in Powell. Is everything all right?"

"It's fine, thanks." Afina was relieved they hadn't mentioned her and also Luke had hopefully persuaded them there was no point in trying to contact Powell at least for the next couple of weeks so with a bit of luck they would stay away from the bar. "Let me know tonight if they say anything else of interest. I'm going to shoot off early as my friend has just left hospital."

"Will do," Luke agreed and returned to his work.

Afina was conscious she needed to warn Powell about Gheorghe but she didn't want to add to his troubles when he needed to be focused on recovering the children. At least while he was out of the country, he was safe from Gheorghe and his friends.

Afina slipped out of the rear door of the bar and walked to the nearby taxi rank. It was only a ten minute drive to where Emma and Becky lived. She didn't feel like taking a bus today. She wanted to see Mara as soon as possible and tell her she had seen Gheorghe in the bar,

Afina liked visiting Emma and Becky's home, as it always reminded her of how they had saved her that night by opening their doors to a stranger in trouble, when she was running away from Dimitry.

"You're early," Becky said upon opening the door.

"I didn't want to miss the party."

They walked through to the living room where Mara and Emma were sitting chatting.

"Glad you're here at last," Mara said. "Now we can open the champagne."

"Are you sure you should be drinking alcohol?"

"The doctor said it was fine in moderation."

"You don't do moderation very well," Afina said, joining Mara on the sofa.

"I'll get the drinks," Becky said and headed for the kitchen.

"I'm going to help Becky," Emma said and also left.

Afina took the chance to tell Mara about Gheorghe's appearance at the bar. "Do you think he knows Powell and Danny are the same man?"

"I hate my uncle but he isn't stupid. He may have worked it out and I know he's spoken to Stefan."

"Have you seen him since last week?"

"No but he did call me and said he was looking for a new property for the business as he thought the old one was tarnished by Victor's death..."

"What?" Afina asked, seeing Mara hesitate.

"He said I should take a couple of week's break and then he expected me to help him set up the new business. He said I wouldn't have to fuck anyone for the foreseeable future, unless I wanted to."

"Do you believe him?"

"I think he will give me some time off from fucking while I help him get to know Brighton and it suits him but..." Mara shrugged her shoulders. "It won't stay that way for ever."

"Does he know where you're staying? It's not fair on Emma and Becky if he comes around here causing trouble."

"I told him I was leaving hospital tomorrow, just in case he turned up to collect me. He doesn't know I'm here."

"What are we going to do?"

"Let's talk about it tomorrow. Today, we are celebrating my being alive and leaving hospital. I don't want to think about the future... or the past for that matter."

"We must think about the future. What will you say when your uncle asks where you are living?"

"Stop being so practical. I will lie about where I am staying. He won't care as long as I do what he wants."

"I hope that doesn't extend to sleeping with him?"

"No, he lost interest in me in that way a very long time ago. He liked being the first and enjoyed me while I was very young but not now."

"Good... Perhaps you should move away, somewhere your uncle can't find you?"

"And where would I go? Anyway, I would miss you too much."

"I'm not sure you take this seriously enough."

"My uncle has been in my life for a very long time. I am used to him. It is only since I met you that I have been shot and in danger."

Afina knew that was true. Everyone she had come in contact with since arriving in Brighton had seen their lives upheaved one way or another.

Afina was grateful Emma and Becky re-entered the room at that moment. Emma was carrying a chocolate cake with several lit candles on top. Becky was carrying four glasses of champagne. Emma put the cake down on the coffee table and Becky handed out the glasses.

"A toast," Becky said, raising her glass. "Welcome back Mara."

Everyone touched glasses and sipped at the champagne.

"Wow, this is good stuff," Emma said.

"Very nice," Becky agreed. "Who wants some cake?"

CHAPTER TWENTY THREE

Powell and Jenkins arrived for dinner at the home they had spent so much time watching, with a sense of trepidation. They had debated right up to the last minute whether they should cancel but eventually taken a taxi, which dropped them outside the large double entrance.

The deciding factor in their decision to go was the opportunity to meet the children again. In the near future, they would in effect be abducting the children from their home and father. When it came to convincing the children they should accompany them to the airport and not run in the opposite direction, Powell thought it was going to be beneficial that they knew each other.

Powell buzzed the intercom on the gate and announced their arrival. The doors immediately swung open and as they entered the driveway, Baz was already coming out the front door of the house with a welcoming smile.

"Good to see you again," Baz said. "And in much more pleasant circumstances."

"Yesterday is not something I would like to repeat again," Powell admitted, shaking hands."

"I rather had the opinion yesterday it was not a new experience for either of you."

Powell had expected Baz to ask about their past, given the aptitude for weapons they displayed. They had agreed how they would respond. "Two ex-soldiers," he said smiling. "But in my case it was a very long time ago."

"I thought as much."

"Me more recently," Jenkins said. "I've been working in Oman for the Royal family."

"Well I think then I was indeed fortunate that you chose yesterday to go shopping. Let's get out this heat and go in the house but may I ask you please not to speak of yesterday's events in front of the children. They had nightmares last night and they are saying they are scared to go out. They didn't even want to go for ice cream tonight!"

Powell remembered for the first time that it was Saturday and their plan for grabbing the children relied on them visiting the ice cream parlour the following Saturday.

"We understand," Powell said. "Hopefully they will get over it quite soon."

"I hope so," Baz said, leading the way into the house. "You must come and meet my wife."

Powell was shocked by the revelation Baz had already married again. He certainly hadn't wasted anytime moving on with his life.

As they entered the house, Powell sucked in his breath at the opulence of the home. He looked across at Jenkins who seemed a bit in awe of his surroundings.

There were marble floors covered with what looked to be very expensive rugs. In the large entrance hall was a huge chandelier and an impressive, wide staircase leading upstairs. The walls to the side of the staircase were covered with pictures of Arab men. Powell wondered if they were family portraits.

Powell had realised it was quite a large house but the plain brick walls outside gave no hint of the impressive interior. It was evident Baz was not short of money.

"You have a beautiful home," Powell said.

"Thank you. It has been the family home for many years. I now live here with my parents."

Baz led the way into the Living room where he introduced his wife and parents who all spoke some English. They were obviously a well-educated as well as wealthy family. The women were wearing full length abayas so it was difficult to determine exactly what Baz's new wife looked like. She was slim and had pretty eyes. Powell suspected she was a few years younger than Baz.

As Powell looked around the room, he came to the view the furnishings wouldn't have looked out of place in a Palace. A veritable feast was laid out on the dining table at one end of the room.

"This looks amazing," Powell said. Despite the surreal situation, he was actually looking forward to tasting local cuisine which he suspected would be of a high quality.

"You are special guests and I told you my cook is excellent. I'm only sorry I cannot offer you anything to drink as is your English custom."

"That's okay, we quite understand." Powell replied.

"Where do you both live?" Baz inquired.

"I live in Brighton," Powell replied.

"I'm from Wales but living in Stevenage recently," Jenkins answered.

"Have you been to England?" Powell asked.

"I lived there for ten years until about a year ago. I worked at the Saudi embassy in London."

"Are you a diplomat?" Powell questioned, warming to the charade.

"Nothing so grand. Just a lowly bureaucrat."

"And did you enjoy living in England?" Powell enquired.

"I enjoyed many aspects of living in England but not your weather."

"Join the club," Jenkins said.

"Why did you leave?" Powell asked.

"My assignment was up and I was missing home. As you English say, home is where the heart is. Now let us eat and you can tell me all about yourselves."

The food was excellent and the finished plates were removed by two servants of Asian origin, who efficiently came and went without being noticed.

"Are you married?" Baz asked Powell while Jenkins was speaking to the grandparents.

"I was but my wife died twenty years ago."

"I am sorry to hear that. How did she die, if you don't mind my asking?"

"She was killed by Irish terrorists."

"That is terrible. We are fortunate we did not also perish in the same way."

"How long have you been married?" Powell had been wanting to ask and now Baz had afforded him the perfect opportunity.

"Just two years. I am a lucky man."

Powell was confused. According to Angela Bennett they had still been married and living together in England twelve months ago.

Have you never thought to marry again?" Baz continued.

"I haven't met the right person."

"And is your friend married?"

"No, Jenkins is also single."

"In our culture it is very important for a man to be married. Women are not so available as in the West and our laws are very strict. No marriage means no fun, if you get my meaning?"

Powell understood perfectly. Sex didn't happen outside of marriage.

Baz continued, "In a few years I will probably take a second wife. It is our custom that when one wife becomes older, she should move onto the household duties and a younger wife is better for keeping the bed warm."

"How many wives can you have?"

"The Quran says I can have up to four wives at one time but frankly I think that is excessive. They are expensive and likely to gang up on you!"

Powell was tempted to laugh but didn't want to be so impolite. There was no doubt sexism was alive and flourishing in Saudi.

"What happened to the mother of Karim and Laila?"

"Sadly she was killed in a car accident. It is one of the reasons I decided to return to live in my homeland."

Powell wasn't surprised to hear Baz's lie, he had worked out that he would have had to tell the children something along those lines. It helped further convince him, he was doing the right thing in helping Angela get her children back.

"Can I ask you about something that has been bothering me?" Powell inquired.

"Of course."

"Why did the guards not allow us onto the floor to escape the terrorists. Surely it was a matter of life and death."

"To someone brought up in England, it must seem very strange but from birth we are brought up this way. If you have never travelled and seen anything else of the world, you do not question these things. Thus the guard was only doing what is ingrained in his very being."

"But you were arguing with the guards when we arrived so does that mean you think differently?"

"Do you agree with everything about England? Probably not. At the Mall, I was thinking about something which occurred around twelve years ago. We had a terrible fire at a school in our holy city of Mecca, where our religious police forced schoolgirls back into a blazing building because they were not wearing Islamic headscarves and black robes. Fifteen girls were killed. The religious police even stopped men from trying to help the girls escape from the building. They said it was sinful to approach the girls."

Powell couldn't hide his shock. "Did they believe Allah wanted those children to die for the lack of the right clothes?"

"You live in England so it will be difficult for you to comprehend such behavior. Even the concept of a religious police is completely foreign to your way of life. I am a devout Muslim but I am also a father. My views have changed over the years and if it had been Laila who died in the school fire in those circumstances, I would have been very angry."

Powell had heard enough. When Bella was killed, though it was senseless, she was doing her job and trying to help someone. He was proud of her actions. As a parent, he could imagine how the parents of the dead girls must have felt. They had a chance of escape denied them because of what they were wearing. If he had found the guards responsible, he would have not been able to control his reaction. The more he learned about Saudi, the less he liked the place. He excused himself to visit the bathroom.

CHAPTER TWENTY FOUR

Powell and Jenkins were anxiously sat in the BMW, praying the children would have lost their fear of leaving the house and be wanting ice cream tonight. Powell was reminded of various stakeouts during his days in MI5, more than twenty years earlier, although the success of an operation had never been quite so precariously balanced between the fear of two children leaving the house and their desire for ice cream.

"Shouldn't they be here by now if they're coming?" Jenkins queried.

"I've seen them come a bit earlier and later," Powell replied, trying to sound more relaxed than he felt. Their visas would be expiring in five days and this was therefore their last chance to utilise Plan A and take the children at the ice cream parlour.

"I'll be glad to get out of this country, it's too damned hot," Jenkins complained. "The heat saps all my energy."

Powell shared Jenkins views about Saudi. "I actually look forward to seeing some rain and some grass when I'm back in Brighton. Everything here is concrete and sand." He didn't like Riyadh as a city and it had nothing to do with the people or the rules. It lacked colour or character. Brighton had both and a soul.

They had turned off the car engine and so the air conditioning had stopped working. It was more than uncomfortably hot in the car, it was quickly turning into a furnace.

"Next time you have a job for me, try and make it somewhere civilised," Jenkins pleaded. "If it has to be hot, I prefer Spain or the Caribbean."

Powell thought it quite probable they would work together again but first they had to get home in one piece. "I'll see what I can do," he promised with a hint of sarcasm.

He checked his watch again because despite his upbeat manner with Jenkins, he was worried. They were definitely running late.

"They're here," Jenkins suddenly announced as the familiar car drove into view.

Powell sat forward in his seat. In just a couple of minutes would see the culmination of weeks of planning. He could feel the adrenaline start to course through his body.

They watched the car pull to a stop in front of the ice cream parlour and the passenger door opened as usual. The grandmother stepped out from the car but instead of opening the rear door as usual, she strode purposefully straight into the ice cream parlour.

"Shit!" Jenkins swore. "What now?"

Powell was desperately trying to peer through the darkened windows of the Range Rover to see if the children were inside the car but close up it would be difficult to tell and they were thirty metres away.

"I'm going to risk a look," Powell said. "Get behind the wheel. If I see the kids are inside, I'm going to take possession of the car and we follow through on the rest of the plan."

Powell walked quickly along the pavement with his head turned towards the ice cream parlour and away from the driver of the car. Once level with the car he checked the grandmother was still ordering the ice creams and then stooped to put his face right up close to the rear window. He then kept walking, certain the car was empty apart from the driver.

He had little experience of wearing the long white robe he was currently wearing but as a disguise it worked perfectly. He had been growing a beard for several days and also using a fast tanning lotion, which together, at least at a quick glance, made him difficult to identify as European.

Jenkins pulled up in the BMW at the side of the road after Powell had walked fifty metres and he climbed inside.

"The children weren't in the car," Powell confirmed. "We'll go to Plan B."

"Let's hope they aren't too scared to go to school," Jenkins said, as he accelerated away from the kerb.

CHAPTER TWENTY FIVE

Powell and Jenkins had observed the children being dropped off at school and breathed a sigh of relief. Then they went back to the hotel, where they hired an additional car for Jenkins to drive and then spent a couple of hours swimming and having lunch. Powell telephoned Angela Bennett to check she understood her role in the events about to play out and then they headed back towards the school to take up their respective positions.

Jenkins drove to the side street they had both picked out as the best place for their plan to take effect. Jenkins could see the Range Rover coming down the main road, in no great hurry. It was a journey the driver had made hundreds of times before without incident.

As the Range Rover came close to the side street where Jenkins was parked, he accelerated the brand new Ford he had hired into the main road and intentionally collided with the front wing of the Range Rover. The driver of the Range Rover had seen Jenkins emerge from the side street, swerved and applied his brakes but been unable to avoid the crash.

Jenkins was first out of his car and went to check on the condition of the other driver.

A stream of broken Arabic poured out of the unhappy driver as he stepped from his car but the man was of Asian descent not Arabic. Jenkins gave a small prayer of thanks for their information being correct. Baz's family, as was common, employed a family driver from India.

Noticing he was talking to a European the driver quickly turned to English.

"Did you not see me coming?" the driver inquired.

"I'm terribly sorry," Jenkins apologised profusely. "I don't know what happened. I looked and there was no car coming and by the time I pulled out you were suddenly there. You must have been going very fast."

A few people were gathering around. Conversations were taking place in Arabic between the driver and others. The noise level was rapidly increasing as was the gesticulating of arms. To Jenkins it appeared everyone on the street had a view on who was guilty.

"I was not going fast," the driver replied. "I have witnesses it was your fault."

"I'm not sure but let's not argue. This is a hire car and of course I have insurance. Should we call the traffic police?"

The driver was inspecting the damage to his car. "If we do that then as we are both foreigners, we may spend a great deal of time at the police station, maybe even behind bars while they investigate. No one is injured and it looks like both cars are drivable."

"I have a number my rental company gave me to call in case of an accident," Jenkins volunteered. "I believe they then sort everything out for us."

"That is a good idea," the driver agreed, obviously relieved.

Jenkins had been told that the Najm or traffic police started off with preconceived notions of guilt, based on the driver's birthplace, when an accident involved different nationalities. Saudis were nearly always innocent, Europeans next best and other nationalities such as Indians at the bottom of the pile. Jenkins had counted on the Indian driver not wanting to call the Najm.

"Do you live here in Riyadh?" the driver asked.

"No, I am just here on business. I'm staying at the Four Seasons hotel."

Jenkins took his mobile form his pocket and dialled the number he'd been given by the rental company. He briefly explained what had happened and answered various questions. He gave the person at the end of the phone the registration number of the Range Rover. The call took about five minutes and then he was told everything was in order for him to leave the scene of the accident.

"That was easier than calling the police," Jenkins said.

"Do you have some paper to write down your name and details?" the driver asked. "I need to provide my family with this information."

"I have a pen and paper in the car," Jenkins revealed and took a notebook and pen from the glove compartment of his Ford. He wrote his name, car registration number and rental company name before handing over the piece of paper to the driver. "Is this sufficient information?" he queried.

"What is your phone number?"

Jenkins took back the piece of paper and added his mobile number.

The driver took out his phone and dialled the number and after a couple of seconds Jenkin's phone rang.

The driver was obviously no fool.

"That is fine," the driver confirmed. "Now I must leave, I have to collect the children from school."

Powell was parked exactly where the Range Rover normally parked, waiting for the children. He was wearing normal clothing as he wanted the children to quickly recognise and be at ease with him. He was pleased Saudi schools seemed to run to a strict timetable and the children emerged as they had every other day, exactly on time.

The children started walking down the street as normal and then realised there was no sign of their car. Powell stepped from his car and walked quickly towards the children. He smiled and gave them a friendly wave as he came near.

"Hi guys," he said. "I've been sent to collect you today as your driver had an accident."

There was a brief look of uncertainty on their faces.

"The driver is fine but the car is out of action," Powell explained. "So I volunteered to collect you." He gave them his best smile.

He turned and started walking back towards the car. This was the moment of truth. If the children refused to go with him it was going to become very awkward.

"Come on," he said pleasantly over his shoulder and was relieved to hear the footsteps behind him.

Karim sat in the front and Laila in the back.

"You can choose the music," he suggested to Karim, who immediately reached for the tuning knob.

Powell pulled away from the kerb with a huge sense of relief. He took out his mobile and pressed the speed dial button.

"I have them," he said simply and passed the phone to Karim. "Someone wants to speak to you."

CHAPTER TWENTY SIX

Powell allowed the shocked children to speak with their mother for only five minutes. Karim had seemed numbed by the realisation his mother was alive and well, while Laila had been overjoyed and crying.

Powell needed his phone back as he was expecting to hear from Jenkins. The call came through saying the driver would be at the school in ten minutes to discover the children were missing. Having arrived late, the driver would no doubt frantically search everywhere for the children, in case they had just returned inside the school. It might take him quite some time to suspect anything was truly amiss. Saudi wasn't a country with any history of crimes against children. It meant that Powell had at least fifteen minutes and probably more like thirty minutes head start.

"Where are you taking us?" Karim asked.

"Back to England, to see your mother."

Karim seemed in shock. "My father lied about her being dead. He said she was killed in a car accident."

"Yes, he did. Your Mum has missed you terribly. I'm sure your father loves you but what he did was a terrible thing."

"When can we see Mummy?" Laila asked.

"Hopefully tomorrow," Powell replied. "We are going to change cars in the minute so get ready."

Powell drove into the Al Mamlaka shopping mall and found a space to park on the ground floor.

"Follow me," he instructed and led the way to the Mercedes he had hired that morning from a different hire company to where he hired the BMW.

"Do either of you have mobile phones?" Powell queried.

"No, father won't buy them for us," Laila answered.

Powell didn't want phones being used to track their whereabouts and would have thrown them away so at least one minor problem was easily resolved.

"Get in the back, please," Powell requested, as Karim went to sit in the front again.

Karim was saying little as Powell continued driving but Laila was excitedly asking questions about her mother. Powell handed Laila his phone and told her which buttons to push to call her mother. After a few minutes, she finished speaking and passed the phone to Karim. He was noticeably not overly excited to be speaking to his mother.

"Father will not like what you have done," Karim said, after finishing speaking to his mother. "He will be very angry with all of us."

"Well he will certainly be angry with me and perhaps your mother but there is no reason for him to be angry with you children."

"Daddy is always getting angry," Laila said.

Powell was surprised by Laila's revelation. "Don't you want to go back to England and see your mother, Karim?"

"I am a Muslim," Karim replied. "England is my enemy and the Quran teaches us to kill our enemies."

Powell was shocked by Karim's radical views. He had sounded like he was reciting something verbatim he had been taught in school. Powell had never considered Baz to be extremist, in fact quite the opposite. Although it had suited Baz to revert to his Muslim ways when he wanted a divorce and to keep his children, Powell hadn't suspected him of holding any radical views. In fact, the meal at his house and discussion about the children killed in the fire, suggested he was quite liberal.

"Where did you learn that?" Powell asked.

"The truth is revealed in many ways."

"I bet it was his special teacher," Laila joined in. "He was always having extra lessons."

"What does it matter who taught me this?" Karim asked.

"But what your father did was wrong," Powell stressed. "He lied to you, telling you your mother was dead when she wasn't."

"I'm sure he had his reasons."

"I am your friend, not your enemy, Karim. And the beauty of living in England is it doesn't matter if you are a Muslim or any other religion. We all respect and tolerate each other's differences."

"Then why do the English and the Americans bomb only Muslims?"

Powell thought it best to say nothing further. This wasn't the time for a theological debate with a nine year old boy.

"We are stopping to pick up my friend Jenkins," Powell announced as he pulled into the side of the road. "You remember him."

Jenkins was waiting in the scheduled spot, having arrived by taxi after leaving his damaged hire car at a different shopping mall car park.

"Everything go okay?" Powell asked, as Jenkins climbed in the back of the car.

"Like clockwork," Jenkins answered. "Hello Karim, Laila. Good to see you again."

"Hello Jenkins, it's good to see you again as well," Laila replied.

Karim's greeting was a more muted, "Hello."

"I had to give the driver my mobile number so I left my phone in the back of the taxi," Jenkins explained. "Hopefully, if they try and locate it, they'll be chasing all over town trying to track the taxi." They had both purchased new pay as you go mobiles specifically for the operation so Jenkins wasn't bothered about the loss of the phone.

"That might cost them a bit of time." Powell said, hopefully.

"I bet you're excited at the prospect of seeing your mother again," Jenkins suggested, turning to the children.

"I'm very excited," Laila responded. "But Karim is being boring as usual."

Powell looked in his rear view mirror and gave Jenkins a slight nod of the head to say, leave the subject alone.

"You know Karim, once you are back in England with your mother, your father will be able to visit you." Powell doubted he was being honest but in theory it might be possible.

Karim said nothing, just sat deep in thought.

"I need you guys to understand a few things," Powell continued. "We are on our way to the airport where we will be catching a flight to England but we are going to stop on the way first for some food."

"Can we choose what we eat?" Laila asked.

"You can have anything on the menu," Powell promised.

"I'm not hungry," Karim said, grumpily.

"It is very important at the airport that you both pretend I am your father," Powell explained, ignoring Karim's moody attitude. "I have new passports for all of us. Your new surname is Smith." Another debt he owed to Brian. "You have been on your summer holidays and now I am taking you back to England to see your grandparents before you then go back to boarding school. Karim, you are now Simon Smith. Laila, you are Chris Smith."

"I don't like the name Simon," Karim moaned.

"You'll only have it for a couple of days," Powell replied pleasantly, but actually irritated by Karim's attitude.

"Is Chris short for Christine?" Laila queried.

"Actually, it's short for Christopher. Laila, you have a very important role in our plan. We are going to pretend you are a boy. Do you think you can do that?"

"I suppose," Laila answered uncertainly.

"The police will be looking for a boy and a girl not two boys," Powell explained. "We are going to play a big trick on everybody."

Laila beamed, "I guess it will be fun."

"Where is our mother?" Karim asked. "Why isn't she travelling with us?"

"She has been taken ill suddenly and can't fly so we are travelling by ourselves. I don't expect you to be asked any questions but just in case, remember your name is Smith and you go to boarding school in England. You spend your holidays here in Saudi. This is really important if you ever wish to see your mother again."

"What if we are found out?" Karim asked.

"Then you will go back to your father as before. You have done nothing wrong." Powell felt Karim seemed less than enthusiastic about everything.

"And what would happen to you?"

"Jenkins and I would probably spend the rest of our lives in jail."

"That's not fair," Laila said.

"And it's not going to happen, not if you both do exactly as I ask you."

CHAPTER TWENTY SEVEN

The journey to their destination took thirty five minutes. Jenkins had used the morning to drive out to the Hotel Makarim and book a room for one night. It was only five minutes further to the airport and would serve as their base for the next few hours. There was a pool and restaurant where they could pass some time without the children getting completely bored. If questioned, Powell and his children were visiting his friend who was flying out the next day.

Powell had booked three economy seats on the 12.35am British Airways flight to Heathrow in his real name plus a seat in the name of Jenkins. He had also booked four first class seats on the 12.30am Air France flight to Paris in the name of Smith and Jenkins had a seat in the name of Jones. This was the flight he intended for them to actually take.

He had decided he wouldn't risk flying on a Middle East airline as they might be persuaded to turn back if their presence was detected on board. The BA and Air France flights were both direct flights, unlike many others, which stopped at one of Saudi's close neighbours to pick up additional passengers. However, the key difference as far as Powell was concerned, was that BA took off from Terminal 1 along with all other international flights except Air France, who for some reason operated from Terminal 2 along with Saudia and Middle East airlines.

In the eventuality that the police came looking for them at the airport, booking reservations on the British Airways flight would hopefully attract the police to the wrong terminal. When they didn't turn up to book in for the flight, it might well convince the police the airport was just a diversion and they never intended to leave by plane. By the time the police reached that conclusion, Powell expected to have checked in at Terminal 2 using the passports in the name of Smith.

They were all reliant on Muhammad, the contact they had been given, whose brother worked for immigration and was going to get them through the security checks. Without his help they would be going nowhere. Powell couldn't help but smile at the irony of the name of the man, who held the success or failure of their escape in his hands.

They wouldn't be able to check in for their flight until 9.30pm so had approximately five hours to kill. Powell had considered hiding out in town somewhere and only arriving at the last minute for the flight but he preferred being close to the airport and thus not risk traffic accidents causing delays.

There was also the likelihood of checkpoints being established but that would take time and by then they would be inside the ring. Being so close to the airport would also allow them to check out the Terminal before venturing inside with the kids.

They had purchased all the swim gear for the children and like most kids they enjoyed messing around in the pool despite the strange circumstances, while Powell and Jenkins watched. The pool was deserted as the airport hotel wasn't exactly a tourist destination. It was solely somewhere people stopped for convenience when flying in or out of the country.

After an hour in the pool they all went up to Jenkins' room to shower and get ready for dinner. Powell was keen to fill the time before the flight doing as many normal things as possible with the children. They had a further call with their mother and even Karim seemed in good spirits.

In the hotel's restaurant both children ordered burgers and fries and ate ravenously. Powell and Jenkins ordered steak, fries and salad. Neither of them fancied anything complicated. The rest of the evening would offer more than its share of complexities and both only ate because they couldn't be sure when they would get to eat again. Saudi jails were not renowned for their cuisine. The children had ice cream for dessert and the adults had a coffee.

"I'll take the kids up to the room," Jenkins eventually suggested. "It's time for you to check out the terminal."

"Do you want me to tell Laila you are going to cut her hair?"

"No, it's okay. I'll tell her when we get upstairs."

Powell hoped Laila wouldn't object to her long hair being cut short to aid her disguise as a boy and fit with the passport photos, which had been provided by their mother and doctored by Brian's friends in MI5.

Angela Bennett had said to promise Laila anything she wanted, to convince her to get her cut, including a trip to Disney if necessary. Armed with such ammunition Powell didn't think Jenkins would receive much opposition to the idea.

He glanced at his watch, it was nine twenty. It was indeed time for a first, cautious look to see if the police were out in force at the Terminal. Although in theory they could now check in, they didn't plan to do so for another hour. They had arranged to meet Muhammad at 10.30pm in front of the Starbucks. More than enough time to search for signs of danger.

Powell had a tight knot in his stomach as he walked outside to the taxi rank and asked to be taken to Terminal 2.

CHAPTER TWENTY EIGHT

Powell could see no obvious signs of extra checks being carried out as he walked into the terminal. There were probably cameras everywhere and if someone in a control room was watching everyone entering, then there was little he could do about that as there was no real way to disguise the children.

There were a large number of check in counters, which serviced all flights leaving from the terminal. There were specific counters for first class passengers with very few people waiting in line. There didn't appear to be any additional checks as bags were taken and boarding cards issued.

The general atmosphere was relaxed, although there were a number of policemen walking around heavily armed but he reckoned they were just the normal deterrent to terrorists. During his time in Saudi he had come to realise how seriously they took the threat of terrorism.

He was satisfied everything was operating normally. He located the Starbucks, ordered a Latte and found a seat which afforded a good view of the major part of the terminal and slowly drank his coffee.

His thoughts turned to his daughter and he remembered how he and Bella had sat in airport cafes, drinking coffee waiting for flights to take them away on holiday. They hadn't been away together the last couple of years as she had preferred to go with friends rather than her Dad. Summer holidays were some of his favourite memories of the all too short time they had spent together.

There was nothing to be gained by further delay so he called Jenkins and told him to bring the children. It was time to get the hell out of Saudi.

About fifteen minutes later, Jenkins and the children arrived in the terminal. Jenkins had their two suitcases on a trolley and the children were walking quietly alongside. Powell approached them while casting a further glance around to see if their arrival was being studied by anyone but as far as he could tell, everything was carrying on as normal, which he found unsettling. Surely there should be extra police everywhere checking for men travelling with two children?

"You look great," Powell said to Laila. He was happy to see she looked like a little boy.

Laila just smiled in response.

"We'll check in first and then take a look around the shops," Powell announced cheerfully. He lifted Jenkins' bag from the trolley. "You get to go first," he said.

"Any sign of trouble?" Jenkins inquired, quietly.

"Nothing so far," Powell replied.

"Here goes then," Jenkins said and headed towards the nearest first class check-in counter without looking back.

Karim went to follow Jenkins and Powell said, "Wait just a minute."

It took Jenkins only a couple of minutes to check-in and then he was walking away with his boarding card.

"Our turn," Powell announced.

He hoped he appeared calm on the outside but inside, his stomach was doing somersaults and a million butterflies were causing havoc. He handed their tickets to the man behind the desk and tried his best smile. He put his bag on the weighing machine at the side of the desk.

The man inspected the tickets and looked at his computer screen. Then he looked up at Powell. "Did you not book four seats, Sir?"

"I did but unfortunately my wife has been taken ill and can't travel. Hopefully she'll be able to join us in a couple of days."

The man looked back down at his screen and pressed various keys. He had a further glance up, pressed some more keys then picked up the phone and said something in Arabic before replacing the receiver.

Powell was getting ready to run.

"Is there a problem," Powell managed to ask.

"Just a small one, Sir. I'm sure it will only take a minute to sort out. I have asked for my supervisor."

Powell could do nothing but wait for the inevitable. After a minute, he observed a man walking towards the desk wearing the uniform of ground crew. The two men spoke in Arabic and the supervisor looked at the screen. They were both pointing at the screen and speaking in heated Arabic.

Finally the supervisor looked up and smiled. "Sorry for the delay," he apologised. "You had been allocated seats on the basis your wife was travelling with you, so two seats together and a further two seats behind.

My colleague has been trying to change the seat numbers so you can all sit together as a three but the system was being difficult. I think we have finally managed to resolve matters. Enjoy your flight."

"Thank you," Powell said, feeling like the condemned man given a last minute stay of execution.

The supervisor walked away and Powell accepted his boarding passes like they were winning lottery tickets. He hurried away with the children and headed for Starbucks.

CHAPTER TWENTY NINE

Powell sat down beside Jenkins and the kids. He handed out the drinks he'd just purchased.

"So far so good," Jenkins said. "It all seems a bit too easy at the moment."

"My thoughts exactly," Powell agreed.

"I need the toilet," Karim announced.

"I'll take you," Powell suggested.

"I'm not a baby" Karim said in disgust. "I can take a pee by myself."

"Okay, the toilet is just over there," Powell pointed.

Karim walked away and Powell watched him all the way to the toilet.

"Can I speak to mummy again?" Laila asked.

"Of course you can," Powell answered and took his phone from his pocket.

He listened as Laila told her mother how much she had missed her, how her new name was Chris and her new haircut wasn't too bad. Her hair would soon grow back.

"Karim missed you at first as well but he's changed," Laila said. "I'm sorry Mummy but he isn't coming back to see you."

Powell instinctively glanced towards the toilets. He looked down at the table and noticed Karim had taken his drink with him. Who takes their lemonade to the toilet if they're planning on coming back?

"What do you mean Laila, he's not going to go back? What did he say to you?" Powell demanded, too sharply.

"It's not my fault," Laila responded, close to tears.

Powell took back his phone and said quickly to Laila's mother, "I'll call you back shortly."

Jenkins was quickly out of his seat and heading for the toilets. "I'll go check on him."

"Sorry Laila, I didn't mean to shout but this is very important. Why did you say Karim isn't going back?"

"He thinks he is a man now and he wants to live with Daddy."

Powell glanced towards the toilets and his heart sunk as he saw Jenkins emerge alone. He beckoned him to return.

"Stay with Laila while I look for him," Powell said. "He can't have gone far."

Powell walked quickly but tried not to attract attention. He took a look inside the toilets to confirm what Jenkins had discovered. He spotted a newsagent nearby. Perhaps Karim's disappearance still had an innocent explanation. Powell hurriedly checked for any sign of Karim looking at the books and toys but he was nowhere to be seen. What would a ten year old boy do in these circumstances?

There were several policemen standing around so if Karim had wanted to ask for help from one of them, there was no shortage of opportunity. However, they did look a bit menacing with their machine guns on display and perhaps Karim would be intimidated.

He would want to speak with his father but Powell had checked and he didn't have a mobile phone. There was no sign of any pay phones. Was it that simple? Powell rushed outside in the direction of the taxi rank. There was a short queue and sure enough, towards the end was Karim.

Powell made sure Karim didn't see him approach from behind.

"The taxi driver won't take you anywhere by yourself," Powell said, as he took hold of Karim's arm. "You're too young."

Karim wriggled to be free of Powell's grip. "I don't want to go with you."

Powell could not afford a scene. He almost lifted Karim off his feet as he moved him away from the taxi queue. Once away from prying ears he said, "Look, I can't force you to get on the aeroplane but let's go back to Starbucks and discuss the options. Then if you really refuse to go I won't force you."

Karim looked dubious. "You promise I don't have to go if I don't want to?"

"Yes, I promise. I can hardly carry you on the plane against your will. Let's go talk about it like two grown men."

"Okay," Karim said and started walking back inside the terminal.

There was a look of relief on Jenkins face as they sat back down.

"Let's have another drink," Powell suggested. "It will help us to relax and then we can talk." He looked at Jenkins and gave an imperceptible nod.

Jenkins confirmed everyone's order and went to the service counter.

"The things is, Karim," Powell continued. "Your mother has missed you terribly. What your father did was very wrong. He should have discussed where you live with your mother not just run away with you in the night."

"Isn't that what you are doing," Karim interrupted.

"It's different because your father has been refusing to allow your mother to see you. She was left with no option. She also has a court order, which says you were wrongfully abducted and orders your father to return you to your mother."

Powell let Karim digest what he had said as Jenkins arrived with the drinks. Powell had suggested the children have a hot chocolate this time, with cream and marshmallows.

Karim focused on devouring his drink as if it avoided the need to respond to Powell.

"Your father has treated your mother very badly," Powell continued. "I don't think that you would behave the same way. You are a young man now and if you don't want to live with your mother anymore, I think you should tell her to her face. It is the least she deserves."

"That is just a trick," Karim replied. "If I come to England, I will never be allowed to leave again."

"Please come to England," Laila implored. "Mummy will be so sad if you don't come."

"I'm feeling very tired," Karim said. He was struggling to stay awake.

"Rest for a bit," Powell suggested. "And we'll talk about it more when you wake up."

Karim slunk back in his chair and closed his eyes.

Powell didn't like having asked Jenkins to administer the sleeping pills but there had been no other way. He saw it as a case of the end justifying the means. The dose wouldn't have any lasting effect and in about eight hours Karim would wake from a deep sleep and they would be landing in Paris. They were flying after midnight and the flight crew shouldn't be surprised at someone so young being fast asleep when they board the plane.

"Don't worry," Powell said to Laila. "Karim is coming to England."

CHAPTER THIRTY

"Are you Mr. Smith?" the man asked.

Powell had seen him approach and he was very punctual so there was little doubt about the identity of the man dressed in flowing Arab robes.

"Yes, I'm Smith. Are you Muhammad?" Powell replied, rising from his seat.

"That name will do. I am afraid I have some bad news. I cannot help you tonight."

"What do you mean? We need to be on this plane," Powell stressed. "We've already checked in."

"Be that as it may, I simply cannot help you."

"Do you want more money? I have more if it is necessary."

"All the money in the world will not remove the men from the Interior Ministry, who are currently watching like hawks all the regular immigration officers like my brother. They are double checking passports and they seem particularly interested in Europeans travelling with children." His gaze lingered on Karim and Laila.

"Is there any way we can get on this plane?"

"No. My advice would be to get as far away from here as possible and as quickly as possible. When the airline discovers you have checked in but are not at the departure gate, all hell will break loose. I don't know what you have done but you have definitely upset someone important with friends in high places. My brother says he has never known scrutiny like this."

Powell was genuinely at a complete loss what to do. "I have a lot more money if it helps," he suggested in desperation.

"You are not listening to me, it is not a question of money. Now I must go. If you are still alive in a week and want to try again you know how to contact me." Muhammad abruptly turned and hurried away.

Powell turned to Jenkins, "Did you get all of that?"

"Enough to know we aren't flying tonight."

Powell had just started to believe they were going to get away with their plan and now they were back to square one. The authorities had set a trap, showing no signs of interest in anyone at the airport but strategically placing their men at the one point no one could avoid – passport control. Powell knew they would have easily been identifiable even with the proper passport stamps. The authorities were no fools, they knew it was possible to buy your way out of the country so they had brought in men who couldn't be bribed.

"We probably still have at least an hour before they come looking for us," Powell said. "I'll carry Karim. Let's take a taxi back to the hotel and collect the Merc."

"Where are we going to stay?" Jenkins asked. "The hotels aren't going to be an option after tonight and the kids need to sleep."

Jenkins was correct in his assertion hotels were off limits. On arrival at any hotel, passports were inspected and photocopied.

"The children can sleep while we take turns driving," Powell replied. "We need to head for Dammam and see if we can get into Bahrain across the causeway."

"Sounds good to me," Jenkins agreed. "Never did like flying, prefer a car journey any day."

CHAPTER THIRTY ONE

Afina awoke and turned over in her bed to try and get back to sleep. She pulled the quilt around her shoulders and tried to ignore the need to have a pee. She glanced at the bedside clock and saw it was three thirty. What an unearthly hour to be awake but she wasn't going to be able to last until morning. She climbed out of bed and was about to head for the bathroom when she froze. There was a sound coming from downstairs as if someone was moving about. She listened intently and heard the sounds again.

Afina reached for her phone, which she kept beside her bed. She dialled the emergency services.

"Which service do you want?"

"Police, please," she said quietly.

"One moment."

Seconds later she heard, "This is the police. How can I help you?"

"I can hear someone moving about downstairs."

"Do you live alone?"

"Yes."

"What's your name and address please?"

Afina gave the information.

"Stay upstairs and try to lock your bedroom door if possible. A car is on its way."

Afina went to her door and pushed the lock closed, trying not to make any sound. There was no longer any sounds coming from downstairs. Then she realised she might have just been very foolish. What if it was Powell downstairs?

She decided to investigate. She looked around the room for any sign of a weapon. Her eyes fell on the iron. It was solid if not ideal. She unlocked her door and crept to the top of the stairs where she stood listening, trying to decipher the sounds she could hear. There was definitely someone in the bar and she didn't believe it was Powell.

If whoever it was thought there was money to steal, he would be disappointed. They didn't leave any money in the bar overnight. It was in the safe in the office. Perhaps it was just a drunk youngster who wanted another drink?

Afina knew with certainty she had locked the doors before going to bed. There was the noise again. Perhaps if she turned on the lights it would cause whoever it was to run away. The best thing was to wait for the police but she didn't like the idea of someone stealing from Powell or maybe damaging his property. She owed him everything and cowering upstairs was not the way to repay him. The bar was her responsibility while he was away.

She turned on the light switch and the stairs were flooded in light. "Who is there?" she shouted. "I've called the police. They will be here in a minute."

She heard the muffled sounds of voices. There were at least two people she realised and wished she had stayed hidden in her bedroom. She held the iron by the cord so she could swing it as a weapon. Anyone coming up the stairs was going to get a surprise.

"Fuck you," she heard someone below shout. "Tell Powell we will be coming for him."

Then there was the sound of feet running away and silence. Despite believing she was alone she decided to wait for the police to arrive. Just five minutes later she heard more people entering the bar.

"This is the police," someone shouted. "Afina are you up there? This is the police."

Afina decided it was safe to venture downstairs. When she reached the bar she saw four uniformed police officers. They were all staring at one wall. Daubed in paint in large writing were the words, BEWARE THIS IS NOT A SAFE PLACE TO DRINK!

One of the officers turned towards Afina. "Probably just kids," he said. "But do you have any idea who else might write this. Have you been having problems with any particular customer?"

"No one I can think of," she lied. She wasn't going to tell him the man who had shouted at her to fuck off, had a strong Romanian accent.

She wished Powell would hurry home. She wasn't just afraid for herself, she was worried for his bar. She didn't want him returning to a business which had lost all of its customers.

CHAPTER THIRTY TWO

The taxi dropped them off in front of the hotel. Powell carried Karim to the Mercedes while Jenkins carried Laila, who had fallen asleep in the taxi.

"I think we should put Karim in the boot at least until we are clear of Riyadh," Powell said. "They are looking for two children and it will give Laila a chance to get some sleep on the back seat."

Jenkins deposited Laila in the car and then opened the boot. He helped Powell gently lower Karim into the spacious boot. Powell provided his jacket as a makeshift pillow.

"I'll drive first," Powell suggested. "You get a couple of hours sleep."

"Fine by me."

They had gone about five miles when they both saw the traffic ahead slowing. Jenkins gave an anxious look at Powell. The cars ahead were now down to a crawl.

"Roadblock?" Jenkins asked.

"Could be an accident."

Two minutes later and they both could see the police cars strung across the road about half a mile ahead.

"What do we do?" Jenkins asked.

"I know what I don't want to do. I'm not spending time in a Saudi jail!"

"I'm of the same opinion," Jenkins agreed. "You should be able to barge through the cars but it's going to get hairy. The kids could end up getting hurt."

Powell was in two minds about what to do. If they were found with the children they would spend a very long time in a Saudi jail. It would mean a failed operation and Angela Bennett would probably never see her children again. If they tried to break through the police roadblock there was a real possibility the children could get seriously injured. Talk about being caught between a rock and a hard place!

"They're looking for two men with a boy and a girl," Powell thought out loud. "We need to change the dynamic of our group."

They were inching slowly forward in the queue of traffic, which was merging into one lane. There were two hundred metres to the checkpoint.

"You need to hitch a lift with someone else," Powell suggested. "There's a European in that taxi," he said, pointing to a nearby car. "Try to stay low so they don't spot you."

Powell was very grateful Jenkins wasn't a man that stood around debating the outcome once he'd been told what to do. He was out of the car and opening the door of the nearby taxi within seconds. Powell had no idea what Jenkins would tell the occupant of the taxi but he was already sharing the back seat with the no doubt very surprised other passenger. The driver would no doubt be very happy with the very large tip Jenkins would provide.

Powell waited just a second to be sure trouble didn't erupt from the taxi and then woke Laila.

"Laila, I need you to do some play acting. Do you like pretend games?"

"Yes," she replied, becoming alert at the idea of a game.

"I want you to pretend you have a very nasty pain in your tummy. Can you do that for me?"

"Of course I can. I sometimes play that game when I don't want to go to school."

"Okay so just stay in the car and try to look very poorly. And remember your name is Chris." Powell gave a big grin as she clutched at her tummy and started moaning.

Powell stepped from the car and walked towards the police men manning the checkpoint. Two officers noticed him coming and pointed at him.

"Do any of you speak English?" Powell shouted as he came nearer. "I have an emergency. My son is ill and needs to get to a hospital urgently."

Powell noticed one of the policemen had evidently understood what he said and appeared to be translating it for the other officers.

"What is your problem?" the officer inquired as Powell arrived at the checkpoint.

"Thank goodness you speak English. I think my son has appendicitis. Can you help me get through this traffic and perhaps give me an escort to the hospital?"

"I'm sorry but we are not able to move from here. We are searching for terrorists."

"Could you at least move us to the front of the queue? Then you can quickly see my son and I are not terrorists. I'm really worried about him."

"Are you travelling just with your son?"

"Yes, we've been to the airport to see some friends catch a flight back to England. Then he started complaining about stomach pains."

"You are English?"

"Yes I am."

"Where are you from in England?"

"Brighton. Do you know it?"

"I studied in London but I have visited Brighton several times. It is a very nice town."

"Yes it is. Look, I really think my son urgently needs medical attention."

The police officer was thoughtful for a second.

"Please help," Powell pleaded.

He had counted there were only four police officers manning the checkpoint. They were all armed but their weapons were holstered. Powell reckoned he had a better than evens chance of being able to take them all out if necessary. The problem would come afterwards when every cop within the vicinity of Riyadh would swamp the area and make escape almost impossible.

The officer suddenly started shouting at his colleagues. Two of them rushed to remove the barrier they had put across the outside lane to force the traffic to merge.

"Drive up this lane," the officer instructed. "And stop here."

"Thank you so much," Powell replied and ran back towards his car.

He manoeuvred his car to the vacant lane and drove to the front of the queue. He stepped out of the car and the officer opened the rear door and looked inside.

"It hurts so bad, Daddy," Laila moaned. "Please stop it hurting."

Powell was certain she had a future as an actress. She was able to play a very convincing sick boy.

The officer glanced around the interior of the car and seeming satisfied, reclosed the door.

"Okay, you can go," the officer said. "Do you know your way to the nearest hospital?"

"I was going to take her to the King Fahad. We've been there before."

"A good choice. You can go and I wish your son a speedy recovery. And say hello to Choccywoccydoodah. It was my favourite place in Brighton for coffee and cake. "

"Thank you, officer. My son also loves Choccywoccydoodah." It seemed slightly surreal, given the circumstances, to be discussing a chocolate shop from back home.

Powell felt he was entitled to speed away and as he looked in the rear view mirror, he saw the officer had already returned to checking other cars.

"Can I stop pretending, now?" Laila asked.

"Yes you can. You did great."

"Will you take me to Choccywoccydoodah? It sounds fun."

"I certainly will," Powell promised.

CHAPTER THIRTY THREE

Powell was relieved when he saw it was Jenkins calling. He had been worried that he might be sitting in a police cell.

"Where are you?" Powell asked.

"My Swedish taxi friend was staying at the Crowne Plaza so that's where I am now, loitering around outside. Where are you?"

"I'm not far from you. I'll come and get you. Be there in about ten minutes." Powell was pleased he'd invested so much time familiarising himself with the city centre.

He finished the call and immediately rang Martin Thwaite.

"Sorry about the late hour," Powell apologised. "Jenkins and I need somewhere to spend the night. Can you help?"

"I'll tell them to expect you at the gate."

Powell liked that Thwaite didn't ask unnecessary questions like, 'why not just book into a hotel?' Powell wondered if he was perhaps a bit more than just an average banker.

"Thanks, we'll be there in about twenty minutes."

Relieved he had at least a temporary solution for the night, he went to the boot of his car and checked on Karim who was still fast asleep. Laila had resumed sleeping on the back seat.

It took less than ten minutes to reach Jenkins.

"Good to see you again," Jenkins said with a big smile, as he climbed into the passenger seat. "

"And you. Luck is on our side at the moment."

"Long may it last. Where do we go now?"

"We're staying at Martin Thwaite's tonight."

"That's a relief. I reckon we have possibly another half an hour before they realise we weren't on that plane and come looking for us."

They spent the ten minute journey to the compound updating each other on how they had made it through the police checkpoint.

It was eleven thirty when they finally parked up outside Thwaite's home. Powell glanced around to make sure no one was about and then lifted

Karim from the boot and hurried inside.

The children were put in the spare bedroom and then Tessa made some tea.

"Sorry we can't offer anything except tea," Thwaite apologised. "You both look as if you could do with something much stronger."

"We're just grateful to have somewhere to rest for the night," Powell said. "It's been quite a day."

"I must admit I wasn't expecting you to turn up with two children. I assume you are in trouble so I'd be keen to know what I've got myself into by letting you stay. For a start, where are the parents?"

Powell decided there was no longer any good reason not to share the truth. "Twelve months ago, their Saudi father, who was married to an English woman, abducted them to live here. He told the kids their mother was dead."

"So you two were sent to get them back?"

"That was the general idea."

"Well done," said Tessa. "The poor mother must be going through hell."

"It's good of you to help," Powell said.

"I was asked to look out for you if I could be of any help," Thwaite stated. "I assume your presence here signifies everything hasn't gone according to plan."

"Sadly true. I had a contact who was going to get us through the airport tonight but the security services were crawling all over the place and no amount of money could motivate him to help us."

"Do you have a backup plan?"

"Not really. I think our best bet is to get across the causeway to Bahrain."

"Do the authorities know it's you two who took the kids?"

"If they don't yet, they should figure it out quite soon."

"It's a five hour drive to Bahrain and then you will still need someone to get you past Saudi passport controls."

"Do you think Lara might be able to help them?" Tessa asked.

"Lara already put me in touch with the guy at the Embassy, who provided the airport contact," Powell explained. "I can try him again for a contact at the causeway."

"Lara may be able to help in other ways," Thwaite suggested. "I think she has shall we say, a closer relationship to certain useful factions at the embassy than I do."

"Is she dating someone at the embassy?"

"Look, I've signed the Official Secrets Act and shouldn't be saying anything but when I'm asked to provide some insight into the economy or banking matters, it's Lara who liaises between me and the Embassy."

"Are you saying she works for the Intelligence Service?"

"I have no idea who exactly she works for but I was invited to the Embassy about a year ago and asked if I was willing to do a service for my country. I was informed Lara would make the requests and take back my responses."

"I know it's late but can you give her a call and invite her over?"

CHAPTER THIRTY FOUR

Martin and Tessa had gone to bed after making everyone some coffee. Powell, Jenkins and Lara were sat around the dining table.

Powell thought there was no point in beating around the bush. "We need help and I believe you are more than just a school teacher."

"I think Martin has said more than he should."

"Look, I used to work for the Security Services in my twenties. It's through old contacts I was given this job."

"I can't say I'm surprised. You didn't seem like banking types."

"Let me explain what's happened over the last twenty four hours, then you can see if you can help or not."

Powell took ten minutes to tell the story of recent events.

"You've caused quite a stink," Lara revealed, when he'd finished. "Abdul Rashid is quite high up in their Intelligence community. I heard on the grapevine something was afoot but I didn't realise you guys were involved."

"I thought Baz just worked for their consular service, rubber stamping passports."

"That was his cover while he was in England. Listen, I shouldn't tell you this but we suspect him of being linked to the funding of ISIS, which is why he is being closely monitored."

"But he was present during the mall attack, surely he would have known to stay well away if he was linked to ISIS?"

"That was probably just bad luck. He's not involved in their daily operations. He's responsible for funds reaching the terrorists. Although Saudi is now the target of bombing at mosques and malls, the fact is they are also the biggest funders of ISIS."

"Angela Bennett described her husband as very western in his views and I would have to agree. We've been to his house and he didn't strike me as remotely what I would call radical."

"I've met him a few times at embassy parties. I agree he does seem very western in his attitudes but that just makes him a good actor."

"So you working in the school is just a cover?" Powell asked.

"It's not just any school. Some of the highest officials send their children to the school to get a good education and prepare them for going to university abroad. It's a good place to make contacts."

"Do the Saudis know what he does?"

"We don't share this type of information with them. We want to turn him and use him in the future. We think that is more valuable than the Saudi approach. They would just haul him off to jail and torture him until he told them everything he knew before having him executed. He's no use to us dead."

Powell understood that developing assets was the name of the game. In his time it had been Catholics willing to provide information about the IRA. Today it was all about Al Qaeda and ISIS.

"I'm worried about Karim," Powell revealed. "He was sprouting quite radical thoughts when we first took him and saying he didn't want to go back to England."

"That is interesting. It helps confirm everything we suspect about Baz. Perhaps his influence is rubbing off on his son. We know Baz isn't helping ISIS for the money, his family is very wealthy, so he must be a true sympathiser."

"Or perhaps he is being blackmailed?"

"It's a possibility but we don't believe it to be the case. At least, we have no evidence to support such a theory at the current time."

"So like father, like son."

"Seems that way. You might not just be returning kids to their mother but saving the world from a future terrorist."

"If I'm to do that I need to get the children out of the country. Can you help?"

"Normally I would say I can get you across the causeway but I think you need to lie low for a few days and let things get back to normal. Otherwise you might just experience the same result as at the airport."

"And where do we stay in the meantime? It's not fair on Martin and Tessa to ask to stay here."

"You can stay with me. It will be a squeeze but if asked, I will pretend you are my brothers, niece and nephew arrived from England. But no one will ask any questions. The guards on the gate are especially chosen to be able to ignore everything that goes on around them in the compound. The authorities don't want trouble with the expatriate community."

Powell glanced at Jenkins. "What do you think?"

"I haven't any better ideas."

"Okay, let's leave the children to sleep now and tomorrow we can move to your place. We shall have to be careful with Karim. He should not be left alone with anyone as we can't trust what he will say. Keep him away from phones as well."

"Agreed," Lara said. "I'm afraid none of you will be able to go out until I make the arrangements for your exit. I'll have Tessa bring you over tomorrow when I get home."

"Thanks for your help," Powell said. "I'm not sure what we would have done without you."

"I'm sure you would have thought of something. You seem quite resourceful. Rest up and I'll see you all tomorrow."

CHAPTER THIRTY FIVE

It was lunchtime and as usual Afina was working in the bar. She had organised for the graffiti to be removed the very next day and business hadn't been affected.

Since the incident, she had been very alert to new people entering the bar and informed all the staff to let her know of anything suspicious. The staff had all seen what was painted on the walls and her request therefore made complete sense and didn't need any detailed explanations about Gheorghe and his friends.

She immediately recognised the two men who entered as the same men who had previously visited with Gheorghe. She alerted Luke as they were sat at one of the tables he covered.

"They are the same men you told me about before." Luke stated. "Did they have anything to do with the painting of the walls?"

"I honestly don't know but it's possible."

"We should call the police."

"And tell them what? Two men have just entered our bar and ordered some food and drink."

"I'll go serve them and see what they want."

The next hour passed quietly enough. Afina kept out of the way of the two men but unlike Gheorghe, they had never met. She hoped she just appeared like any other bar girl going about her work.

Luke reported that they ordered food but on this occasion asked no questions about Powell.

Afina was starting to think they were doing no more than keeping an eye on the bar when she heard the raised voices coming from their table. She could see Luke was talking to the two men, who were obviously complaining about something.

"I'm not paying for this food. It was terrible," one of the men shouted so the whole bar could hear.

"I'm sorry you didn't like it, Sir," Luke answered, politely. "Would you like something else?"

The man stood up and threw the plate on the floor. The people at the adjoining tables turned in shock at the impact of the plate smashing on the wooden floor. Pieces of the plate flew in all directions.

"Hey, watch what you're doing," one young man at an adjacent table warned. He was with a pretty girl who had jumped up from the table and was checking her leg where a fragment of the plate had cut her skin.

Luke took a few steps backwards. The two men were intimidating in their size and manner. No one in the bar had any doubt they were dangerous.

Afina reached for her mobile and called the police. Then she approached the two men. "The police will be here in a minute. Get out and don't come back."

"This place is crap," the second man said, standing. He also threw his plate on the floor, with similar noisy consequences from the plate crashing and people complaining.

"Get out," Afina screamed.

The man moved surprisingly quickly for someone so big. He swung his hand and slapped her with his palm, flush on her cheek, sending her flying backward to the floor. The noise was heard by everyone and several men rose to their feet intent on helping.

Two men in particular advanced towards the troublemakers.

"The lady asked you to leave," one of them said, firmly in a foreign accent. He was of average build and dwarfed by the two men he was confronting.

His friend was on his knees checking on Afina.

"Piss off," the man who had hit Afina swore.

The diner took a step forward but before he could say anything further he was shoved squarely in the chest, propelling him backwards against a nearby table, causing further crockery to fall to the floor.

"Don't eat here," the original man to complain shouted loudly. "It will be bad for your health."

Both men then turned and hurried away. On the way out they tipped up two tables they passed, sending crockery and food flying all over the floor.

Afina was helped back up by a combination of Luke and the man who had gone to her aid.

"Are you alright?" Luke asked, concerned.

"I'm okay." She tried to smile as she noticed all eyes in the bar were staring in her direction. "I apologise for the disturbance. Please all have a drink with our compliments."

Afina's face stung like hell but she was more concerned for the mess all over the floor. "Luke, get the floor cleaned, please."

"Of course. Do you want me to call the police?"

"I've already called them. Just get this place cleaned up."

The man who had been shoved backwards walked up and also inquired, "Are you sure you're okay?"

"I'm fine. Thank you for helping."

"I didn't do much. By the way, my name is Gilles."

"I'm Afina."

"This is Johny," he said, indicating his friend, who was picking smashed plates off the floor.

"We haven't been here before, is it always so exciting?" Gilles inquired with a smile.

"Fortunately not. Have you eaten yet?"

"Yes, we just finished our meal."

"Then take a seat at the bar and let me buy you a drink. I'll join you in a minute."

"That would be nice," Gilles replied and headed for the bar along with Johny.

Afina went to the tables that had been upturned and helped the diners pick them back up. Other staff snapped out of the trance, which seemed to have enveloped them and rushed up to help.

"Lunch will be on us today," Afina announced. "And the next time you visit."

The diners all offered their sympathy and seemed far more concerned about Afina's welfare than their spoilt meals.

"I'm fine, really," she confirmed. "Give your orders to the staff and we will rush them through. Order anything you want from the menu."

She joined Gilles and Johny at the bar. "Thank you for intervening. It was very brave of you both. What would you like to drink?"

Gilles ordered a brandy and Johny a beer.

"I hope this doesn't hurt business," Johny said.

"Do you own this place?" Gilles asked.

"I am just the manager. The owner is abroad. Where are you from Gilles?"

"I'm French. What about you?"

"I'm from Romania."

"If you have any damage, we would be glad to help you fix it," Johny offered. "We have a hardware store in Woodingdean." He took a card from his pocket and handed it to Afina.

"Johny's Wares," Afina read out loud. "Thank you. I will call you if I need anything. I hope you will come again and lunch will be on us next time."

"We will definitely come again," Johny promised.

It took ten minutes for the bar to return to something like normal and then Afina felt she could go to the office for a minute. There was still no sign of the police. Someone not paying their bill was obviously not very high on their priorities.

She slumped in the chair and felt like crying but held back her tears. She needed to talk to Mara.

CHAPTER THIRTY SIX

Karim had awoken particularly confused how they had been in the airport one minute and in Thwaite's house the next. Fortunately, he had no suspicion of having been drugged. Powell explained briefly that he had fallen asleep at the Starbucks just before the change of plan, which was the result of too many police at the airport checking passengers, as they went through passport control. They had decided they would drive to safety instead. Karim seemed embarrassed that Powell had needed to carry him to and from the car, and asked no further questions.

Lara had come home from school at lunchtime feigning a bad headache and Tessa took them all across to her house. Both Karim and Laila seemed to like Lara. Karim in particular seemed to appreciate that she spoke Arabic. The children had only the clothes they were wearing so Tessa offered to go shopping. They needed all the basics such as toothbrushes as well as a change of clothes.

Tessa returned laden down with presents for the children. There were all of the essentials they needed plus a good collection of games for them to play. Karim was particularly excited by the arrival of chess, especially when he discovered Jenkins liked to play. He had been learning for the past year and admitted he had never beaten his father but doubted Jenkins was as good.

The rest of the day passed in good humour. The children enjoyed not having to go to school and played various games with Jenkins, who had an insatiable appetite for competing at everything from chess to scrabble. Even Karim seemed to have lost his sharp edge and when he spoke with his mother, promised he would be coming back to England.

The house had three bedrooms. The children were in the second double room and having won the coin toss, Jenkins was in the small third room, leaving Powell to the sofa downstairs. Lara cooked a simple pasta dish for dinner and the children went to bed in good spirits.

Powell wasn't feeling so positive. He felt like a caged animal as he paced the small living room. He felt trapped and didn't like the operation having spiralled out of his control. He was now reliant on Lara and though he was attracted to her and she seemed very capable, it wasn't how he liked to operate.

The others having gone to bed, Powell chose a book to read from Lara's bookcase as he didn't yet feel like sleeping. He'd had difficulty sleeping since Bella's death or more precisely, he found it difficult to fall asleep.

He finally drifted asleep but not long later was awoken by the sound of footsteps approaching his sofa. The person was trying to walk quietly and avoid detection. Powell prepared himself to respond to the intruder.

"Are you asleep?" Lara whispered.

Powell opened his eyes and replied with a smile, "I almost was."

"Sorry but I couldn't sleep knowing you were down here."

Lara was wearing pyjama shorts with a matching t-shirt. Powell could see that her nipples were erect and she was wearing no bra.

"I guess my hormones are working overtime," she continued. "I don't get to spend much time with any man I find attractive. Actually that's zero time."

She knelt down beside the sofa and kissed him on the lips, lightly at first then more hungrily. Powell quickly responded and pulled her closer. He half wondered if he was dreaming as he reached for her breast and played with her nipple through her t-shirt.

He was wearing just his boxers and she slid her hand down his chest and under the elastic of his shorts. She sent an electric shot through his body as she touched his already hardening cock. He groaned as she started to gently stroke his cock and moved her lips to his chest and slowly down his body, giving a mixture of soft kisses and small licks. He could feel her hot breath on his skin and his heart was beating fast in expectation.

She took him in her mouth and ran her tongue around the top then down the shaft. She teased him with further flicks of her tongue before finally taking all of him deep in her mouth. He moved his hips off the sofa, encouraging her to take him even deeper. It was a feeling he hadn't experienced for a very long time. A beautiful woman was freely offering up her mouth and throat to his desires rather than for payment, as had been the case with Mara and Afina. The whole experience felt different.

Powell sat upright as Lara continued to move her mouth up and down his cock. He pulled her t-shirt over her head, forcing her to stop sucking for a moment. In the semi darkness, he caressed her naked breasts as she again took him deep into her throat, causing her to gag a little. She withdrew slightly, then returned determined to take all of him. He enjoyed the sensations for a few seconds but he had no intention of allowing himself to finish too quickly. He pulled her face back up to his so he could kiss her further and explored her mouth with his tongue.

After a minute of passionate kissing, he laid her down on the sofa and pulled off her shorts so she was completely naked. He started by kissing her neck, wanting to slowly build the anticipation. Then he moved to her breasts, where he circled her nipples with his tongue before taking them each in turn in his mouth, sucking and nibbling on them.

Lara was moaning softly and he moved downwards, spending time kissing the contours of her body. When he reached her thighs he teased her until she began to move her hips in a desperate attempt to have his tongue sate her need to feel his touch. Eventually he satisfied her desire by finding her clit and licking gently in a circular movement. His tongue found her already wet and open as she encouraged him to explore all of her. At the same time his hands stretched upwards to find both her nipples.

The combination of his tongue and his hands was having the desired effect and Lara was writhing on the sofa looking for satisfaction. He changed position and replaced his tongue with his cock. As he entered her, she moaned and began to move in rhythm with his thrusts.

"That feels so good," Lara said appreciatively. "Fuck me, Powell. Please fuck me."

Powell kissed her nipple and tugged on it as he withdrew on each stroke.

Lara was gripping his buttocks tightly. "Harder, Powell. Harder."

Powell was conscious of the others upstairs and tried to smother her lips with kisses, hoping to stop her waking everyone.

Lara was panting faster. "I'm going to cum," she cried out, pulling away from his kisses.

Powell had been so focused on giving Lara her orgasm, he was still some way from his own climax as she held him tightly and her body shook with the waves of pleasure.

She took a minute to relax. "That was really good," she acknowledged. "Sorry I was so quick. It's been a while."

"It was perfect." Powell realised it was the first orgasm he had given any woman in a very long time and it made him feel very good about himself. He realised he much preferred mutual satisfaction to the experience of paying for sex, where all the focus was only on his pleasure.

"It was perfect for me," Lara confirmed. "Now it's your turn. How do you want me?"

For an answer, Powell moved his cock towards her mouth.

CHAPTER THIRTY SEVEN

"Can we go for a swim today?" Laila asked at breakfast.

Powell knew the children were going to go crazy stuck in the house all day. "Okay we'll all go for a swim mid-morning," he conceded. There was an element of risk but there would only be a few expatriate wives at the pool as everyone else was at work so it should be relatively safe.

Lara had already left for work. He had seen her briefly when she came downstairs but she was running late and not stopped for breakfast. She was wearing a simple black abaya but if it was meant to cool male passions it didn't work for him as he remembered the feel of her naked body.

"Did you sleep alright?" Jenkins inquired, interrupting his thoughts.

"Fine, thanks." Powell wondered if there was a hint of something in the way Jenkins asked. Had he heard them last night?

"How long do you think we have to spend here?"

Powell turned towards the children. "Why don't you go upstairs and get your swimming costumes on," he suggested. Once they had left the table he answered Jenkins' question. "Lara says the best time to drive across the causeway is Thursday night when thousands do the same for the weekend."

"That means another three nights here. I was thinking that if they put everything together and come looking for us in our real names, which they will have done by now unless they're really useless, then they are going to discover your business trip was sponsored by the bank. That's going to lead them to Martin Thwaite, which is a bit too close to here for comfort."

"I think Martin can expect a visit today at the bank but our cover story is solid. He won't be implicated and he's very senior so won't easily be intimidated. He'll just profess ignorance of anything except our meeting."

"I guess we're lucky to have somewhere to stay... And that Lara is a beautiful woman."

"She certainly is," Powell agreed, wondering again if Jenkins was trying to extract something from him. There was no way he was admitting to Jenkins, anything about the previous night.

Powell's phone rang and he saw it was Angela Bennett calling. He knew she was in a fragile state of mind. She had expected by now to be with her children. When he'd called last night to say they wouldn't be on the plane she had almost had a breakdown. He had assured her the children were safe and it was a temporary delay but been unable and unwilling to give her any more details.

"Hello Angela," he greeted her. "Do you want to speak to the children?"

"In a moment. I just had a call from Baz."

Powell could hear in her voice that she was struggling to stay in control. "What did he say?"

"That he knew who had his children and you would never leave Saudi Arabia alive. He also threatened me. He said if I didn't tell him where you were hiding, he knew where to find me and would bring some friends to punish me. He asked if I knew that they still stoned women to death in his country."

"He is just trying to scare you," Powell reassured her. "But just to be safe, could you move into a hotel. Somewhere near Heathrow would be best. Don't tell a soul where you are going. It will only be for a few days."

"As long as that. I was hoping you would be back today."

"It's best we lie low for a few days. You've waited twelve months to see them so a few days more won't hurt."

"I'll never be able to repay you for this."

"I think the expression on your face when I handover your children will be payment enough. Now let me get the kids on the phone."

CHAPTER THIRTY EIGHT

It was late afternoon when Powell received a call from Brian.

"To what do I owe this pleasure?" Powell asked.

"I've just had a very interesting conversation with my boss. He was basically officially warning me off helping you or interfering in Saudi affairs."

"What does that mean?"

"Fortunately we have a very good relationship. After the official warning he hinted we were interfering in an Intelligence Service operation."

"What had you told him about my operation?"

"Nothing so I was somewhat surprised when he knew as much as he did. I would guess MI6 doesn't want you causing trouble for our allies, which I warned you would be the case but there's probably more to it than that."

"There is indeed. It seems the spooks suspect Baz of working with ISIS."

"That would explain everything. Don't say anything else over this line, just in case someone is listening. For my boss to even know you are out there means someone over there has been feeding back information about you. Any idea who that might be?"

"Possibly, I did have to get some help from someone at the embassy." If someone was listening, Powell didn't want to be naming Lara or anyone else.

"Tread carefully," Brian warned. "The spooks don't like people treading on their turf."

"I promise I'll watch where I plant my size twelves… You know, it's strange to think how the job has changed since our days in the field. I remember rushing around trying to find a telephone box to call for backup. Your life could depend on whether the local kids had vandalised the phone box. How the hell did we ever survive?"

"On our wits."

"I guess in that respect nothing has changed."

"I'll be buying the drinks next time we meet," Brian promised. "I suspect you will have quite a thirst by the time you return."

"I will indeed."

Powell didn't have time to dwell on the call as he heard a car door slam and looking out the window saw a taxi was depositing Lara back home. He decided he wouldn't mention the call with Brian. It would be unfair and sound ungrateful to challenge Lara about what information she had fed back to her bosses. She would have had to file a report.

He filled the kettle to make coffee.

"How's your day been?" Lara asked as she entered the kitchen.

"Not as good as my night was."

Lara's face broke into a big grin. "Same here."

"I can't get used to seeing you dressed like that," Powell admitted, referring to the black abaya Lara was wearing.

"I found it strange when I first arrived but I'm used to it now."

"I can barely tell it's you inside."

"So I don't turn you on dressed like this?"

"I wouldn't go as far as to say that!"

"How are the children?" Lara inquired

"They're fine. We took them for a swim to let off some energy."

Lara looked concerned. "I'm not sure that was a good idea."

"It was the lesser of two evils."

"Where are they now?"

"In the lounge, beating Jenkins at Monopoly."

"I have to go out later," Lara said. "The restaurant does takeaway pizza, if that's all right for dinner tonight?"

"Sounds perfect."

She took a menu from the kitchen drawer. "See what the kids want."

"Is your going out to do with us being here?"

"Yes, I'm meeting a contact who can help organise the stamps you need at the causeway."

"Do you want me to come with you?"

"No, its best I go alone and frankly I don't want to risk being seen with you."

"I understand." Powell detected a slight hesitation on Lara's part as if she was unsure whether to say something. "What else?" he prompted.

"Muhammad's been taken into custody. They probably scoured the airport CCTV and found film of him speaking with you. They'll be interrogating him now to find out what he knows and when I say interrogate, they don't hold back with their methods. He will tell them everything he knows."

"He doesn't know anything important," Powell confirmed. He felt guilty he was responsible for a man who was trying to help them now being tortured. Then again, he wasn't really responsible. Muhammad had made his own choices. Charging money to illegally get people out of the country was always a risky proposition.

"It means they now have evidence of your involvement and your pictures are probably being circulated amongst the police. Thus I don't think you can afford to leave the house again."

"The compound guards have seen us a couple of times, entering and leaving."

"Expatriates are coming and going every day. They are unlikely to remember one European face from another. They are more concerned with the terrorist threat posed by anyone non-white."

"I guess that makes sense. I'll go find out what pizzas everyone wants."

"One other thing I'd like to order," Lara said. "More of the same I had last night. If that's all right with you."

"That would be very all right with me."

CHAPTER THIRTY NINE

Lara took a taxi to the address in the centre of the city. She was still wearing her abaya, which she did whenever she travelled around the city. Although the average foreign woman would wear modest, western style clothes, which covered her body and a headscarf, Lara chose to wear the black abaya. It was essential for her teaching job and also for her intelligence work. The abaya enabled her to merge into Saudi society without being noticed.

It was the first time they had met in a private apartment and she wondered if he owned it or had just borrowed it for this assignation. Was it somewhere he regularly met many women perhaps? When she accepted the invitation, she was under no illusions about what would take place.

She was a little nervous but also excited. This meeting was the culmination of a great deal of hard work. She knocked on the door and it was quickly opened and she hurried inside, away from prying eyes. The apartment was quite bare on the inside and poorly decorated. She thought it had the look of a safe house rather than somewhere inhabited for day to day use. She hoped there would at least be a decent bed.

"It's good to see you," Lara said in Arabic.

"And you. Let's speak English though. I don't get to practice it enough."

She smiled. "English is good for me."

"I have made some tea. Would you like some?"

"I hope you didn't come here just to drink tea with me," she teased. "Is there somewhere I can change?"

"The bedroom is there," he said, pointing.

"Thank you. I won't be long."

When she opened the bedroom door and walked back into the room, she was wearing only expensive red lingerie. She noticed how he audibly sucked in his breath at the sight of her.

"You look a vision," he said.

"Thank you. Black is not a very flattering colour." She walked across to him and leaned her neck upwards, inviting him to kiss her.

He obliged with a passionate kiss and she was immediately reminded of the kisses she had shared the previous night with Powell.

"I've never done this before," Lara said. "It's been over a year since I had a man."

"What a waste that such beauty should not have been enjoyed by anyone for so long."

His hands started to explore her body, working their way from her back down to her bottom. He pulled her closer and she could feel his erection pushing against her thigh. They kissed and then she stepped back.

She undid her bra and pulled down her knickers, then stood before him fully naked. "I so want you," she said.

He removed his white ankle length thobe. Underneath he was wearing boxers and she could see the bulge signalling his excitement. His body was covered in dark hair and lacked the toned muscles of Powell.

She advanced towards him and knelt in front of him. She slid the boxers down his legs and his cock bounced upwards as it was freed. It wasn't very long but it was quite thick. She took him in her mouth and again her mind went back to the previous night.

"Let's go to the bedroom, " he suggested after a minute.

She playfully ran ahead and jumped on the bed. She opened her legs so he could see all of her exposed as he entered the room. He knelt at the side of the bed and pulled her closer so he could access her fully with his tongue.

Lara enjoyed the sensations she was experiencing and after a few minutes she genuinely wanted him inside her. "Please fuck me," she said simply.

"It will be my pleasure," he replied. "But I have a rule. I am a married man and I do not put my cock in any woman's pussy except my wife's."

He walked to the bedside drawer and she was glad to see him take out a packet of condoms. Then he took out a large dildo which he covered with a condom.

She thought him slightly weird but was happy to see he had come prepared and hell she didn't mind playing with toys. She saw him take out a tube of something which when he covered the dildo with its contents, she realised was lube.

He climbed onto the bed. "Doggy is best," he said.

She moved into position and looked again over her shoulder at the dildo, which was a good eight inches in length and she let out a small involuntary shiver of excitement.

"You'll need this," he said, handing her the dildo.

She was surprised but took it anyway. Then she saw him applying the lube to his cock and immediately knew his intentions.

He put one hand on her hip to hold her firm and with the other hand guided his cock to the entrance to her anus.

He pushed firmly but slowly inside. "Use the toy," he commanded. "I am going to give you a good Arabic fucking."

For a few strokes he was gentle but then was burying himself balls deep. His thickness made it mildly painful but she decided there was no point in holding back. She inserted the dildo and the tightness of having both holes filled at once, quickly had her close to orgasm. It was not something she had ever experienced before.

She moved her hips back to meet his thrusts and the grunting noises he was making warned her, he was about to cum. At the last second he withdrew, tore off the condom and shot his sperm all over her bottom and back. In the same instant she was climaxing and collapsed forward on the bed.

He lay next to her for a minute, out of breath and recovering from his exertions. His hand gently stroked her body.

She had quite enjoyed the sex, although deriving personal pleasure or not from satisfying him wasn't important. There were far more critical factors at play than whether or not she had an orgasm. On balance, the fact she hadn't had to fake it did add a touch of realism and could only be of benefit.

"That was very good," he said.

"It was better than good, Baz," Lara replied. "Hurry up and get your energy back, I haven't finished with you yet. Not by a long way."

Powell had stayed awake, waiting for Lara to return. He was excited by the thought of making love to her again. That was the difference he realised between the recent sex he had experienced. He had fucked Mara and Afina but he had made love to Lara. Not that he didn't think Afina was capable of making love. The circumstances of their meeting had set the parameters for their sex.

Lara had a beautiful body, fuller and more womanly than the younger Afina. Lara was dark skinned and Afina pale with freckles. They couldn't be more different. Both appealed but here and now he could only think of

Lara.

He thought about how his life had changed so much in such a short space of time. He couldn't say it was for the better, not after Bella's death but what he was doing right now, trying to help Angela Bennett, was a great deal more fulfilling than anything else he had done work wise for twenty years.

He heard the front door open and Lara enter the lounge. "Hi," he said. "How was your evening?"

"Different," she answered. "But good."

"The others went to bed about an hour ago."

She sat on the edge of his sofa. "I'm really tired. Do you mind if we put more sex on hold until tomorrow. Work was a bit intense today. I really don't have the required energy tonight."

Powell was disappointed but understanding. "That's okay. I'd rather have you when you're full of energy." In truth, he was quite aroused and had been so looking forward to a repeat of the previous evening's fun, he knew falling asleep was going to be difficult.

She leaned down and kissed him lightly on the lips. "Thanks, I promise to make it up to you. See you in the morning."

Powell watched her walk away and wondered whether the previous night would turn out to be a one off occasion. If it was, he wouldn't complain. After all, he would be leaving within a few days anyway. They weren't going to be able to embark on a normal relationship. Perhaps she had been thinking along similar lines and didn't want any further involvement or complications.

He turned on his side and tried to avoid recalling the previous night's events.

CHAPTER FORTY

Afina had hired additional security to cover the lunchtimes. Previously the bar had only had doormen from seven at night. She wasn't sure how Powell would feel about the additional expense but she felt she had little choice. A second visit from Gheorghe's friends and it was likely the bar would get a bad reputation, which would seriously hurt takings. At the very least, the presence of the bouncers provided reassurance to the staff and regulars.

The police had viewed the CCTV pictures, which clearly captured everything that had occurred. When the police asked if she knew the men, she answered honestly that she had no idea who they were. She didn't think she should open up to the police about Gheorghe before speaking with Powell and she was loathe to worry him while he was in Saudi, desperately trying to rescue the two children. His return had already been delayed, which made her worry he was having problems.

He had phoned briefly, to say he expected to be back within a few days and until then she would say nothing about what had happened. He had entrusted the bar to her safe keeping and she would deal with the problem. Hopefully he wouldn't return to find his business almost bankrupt.

The local newspaper had printed pictures of the two men on their inside page, along with an appeal from the police for the public to come forward if anyone knew of their whereabouts. Afina didn't believe they would dare to make a return visit to the bar.

The problem was that Mara had confirmed Gheorghe could call on many men to cause problems not just a couple. He was the head of a large crime organisation, which at a guess employed more than forty men, all of them capable of extreme violence.

Afina had invited Mara to have lunch with her at the bar so they could talk about the future. It was Mara's first social outing since leaving hospital. Afina sat at a table served by Luke and informed him she was having some time off to enjoy lunch with her best friend. Mara had flirted with Luke and he had been a very attentive waiter.

Afina chose a nice bottle of red wine and they ordered some tapas to share.

"Have you spoken again with your uncle?" Afina asked, once they were alone.

"He called me yesterday and said he wanted to show me the new house he is renting."

"Where is it?"

"Off Western Road again but slightly nearer to Hove."

"So what did you say?"

"I'm going to meet him there tomorrow."

Afina couldn't hide her look of disapproval. "You've only been out of hospital a week. You should be resting."

"I told you before, my uncle is not a man you refuse when he asks something."

"So when he asks you to fuck his friend, you will just do it? Where does it stop?"

"To be honest, I don't know what to do. I am not like you, Afina. I don't want to serve tables. I would prefer to spend one hour fucking a man than all day as a waitress or working in a supermarket, which are the only other type of jobs I could get."

"I'm sorry, I have no right to criticise your choices. It's not you getting paid for having sex I mind, I'm just afraid of your uncle. We are all in danger while he remains here in Brighton. I am scared for myself and for Powell."

"Powell can take care of himself."

"Yes but not if he isn't here. I don't want your uncle to destroy the bar. I've brought Powell more than his share of problems."

"Then we must make my uncle want to return home. If I can persuade him that I can run the business here, then I don't think he will stay very long."

"But that involves trafficking girls like me to work as prostitutes. Girls who are not making a free choice like you, who if offered a choice would probably choose a job in a supermarket every time. You can't seriously say you would be part of that?"

"I'm sorry, I wasn't thinking."

"We need to put a stop to his business."

"Afina, we are not the police. We are just normal girls. How are we going to be able to stop my uncle?"

"We need help, especially with Powell not here. He gave me his friend Brian's phone number to contact in emergencies. I am not sure exactly what he does but he is some kind of policeman. I think this qualifies as an emergency after what has happened to the bar. I'll give him a call and see what he suggests."

CHAPTER FORTY ONE

Powell risked a further visit to the pool with the kids as they were reaching their limits of staying indoors. Fortunately there were no locals allowed around the pool, it was strictly only for the expatriate community.

When Lara returned home from teaching, she seemed to Powell to be in particularly good spirits. She went straight upstairs to change out of her black abaya and came back down in jeans and a bright yellow top. She looked transformed into a different woman.

"You look like the cat who got the cream," Powell said. "You must have had a particularly good day at school."

"I'm looking forward to getting more cream later," she whispered in his ear.

Powell wondered for a second if she had been drinking but that wasn't possible. "Is your good mood anything to do with getting rid of us?"

"Our contact thinks Friday will be possible. He says there were extra security personnel everywhere two nights ago but yesterday it was pretty much back to normal."

"But I thought Thursday was the best time to go?"

"The start of the weekend rush is Thursday evening and that's when most of the single men travel to get an extra evening on the town. The causeway can end up looking like a giant car park. Friday morning is also quite popular, especially with families but there is far less traffic. Most importantly, it is also when our contact will be working the day shift."

It was the best possible news Powell could hear. "How do we get to the causeway?"

"That's still to be finalised."

Powell didn't like the powerless feeling of relying on someone else to organise everything but he couldn't be in better hands. "I guess we'll have to make the most of our last couple of nights together then," he suggested.

"Exactly what I was thinking. I've already dismissed any plans for your exit involving too much walking because you aren't going to be fit to walk anywhere once I've finished with you."

"Promises, promises!"

After dinner they all played card games with the children before putting them to bed. Powell had noticed Karim seemed a little happier at the prospect of returning to England. He had even asked about Arsenal, who he described as his football team. Powell promised to take him to the Emirates stadium once they were back in England, which was met with great excitement.

Whatever radical views Karim had been fed, Powell didn't think there had been time for them to grow very strong roots. He was confident that after a short time spent back in England, Karim would soon forget all radical ideas.

Jenkins still had some of the sleeping powder left but Powell didn't want to use it during the daytime. Karim had thought he was just extra tired at the airport and therefore fallen asleep and slept well. It would have made sense he was in a deep sleep in the early hours of the morning, had they boarded the plane.

Driving to Bahrain, there was the possibility someone would speak to Karim at one of the checkpoints and if he was unable to respond it could be a serious problem. It was important therefore that Karim could be trusted to say the right things. Powell was going to have a final chat with him before they left, making sure he understood the danger they were all in, if he said anything out of place.

Just after eight, Martin Thwaite came over and they all shared coffee.

"I had a visit from the police today," Thwaite announced. "Two of them and they were asking about you two and what exactly you do for the bank. I kept to the script and acted ignorant of everything except what we discussed at our meeting."

"Did they threaten you?" Powell asked.

"No, they were quite civil. The Saudis tread quite carefully with a bank as large as us. We hold the accounts and thus the secrets of many of their oldest families."

"Well I guess that at least confirms they know we are responsible for taking the children," Jenkins said. "Not that it was ever really in doubt."

"I just want to wish you good luck," Thwaite said. He stood to leave and shook both men's hands. "I won't see you again before you leave. I hope everything goes smoothly for you."

"Thanks," Powell replied. "We couldn't have done it without you."

"That bar you have in Brighton. What's it called again?" Thwaite asked.

"Bella's. It's in Hove actually."

"When we get back to England, Tessa and I are going to come and look you up. We shall have at least a couple of weeks holiday before we go out to Singapore and a visit to Brighton won't go amiss. I think we need to have some proper champagne together."

CHAPTER FORTY TWO

Lara was ready to meet again with Baz. It had been two days since their previous meeting. She arrived at the apartment straight from school. She was again feeling nervous but this time for different reasons. Baz was about to receive a huge shock and there was always the possibility of him turning violent.

Baz opened the door and quickly ushered her into the room. Lara had to smile because it was obvious that however much he was looking forward to seeing her, he didn't wish to be seen with her. Well that was true for her as well. From here onwards it would be even more vital that they were never identified as having met in secret.

"It's so good to see you again," Baz said. "Our last meeting was very memorable. I was so happy to hear you wanted to meet again so quickly."

He took her in his arms and was about to kiss her when she pulled away.

"We need to talk," she stated, sternly.

"Okay. What do you want to talk about?"

"Let's sit down," she suggested. She chose to perch on the corner of the table opposite him, rather than sit next to him on the sofa.

"You sound very serious. Is everything alright?"

"I'm afraid I have some bad news for you, Baz. You have fallen foul of a classic honey trap."

His expression changed to a look of horror. "What nonsense is this? What do you mean?"

"You know perfectly well what I mean. Someone as senior as you in your country's Intelligence Service will be very familiar with the term. You have been caught letting your cock rule your brain. A problem common amongst men but in your profession a fatal error."

"Who do you work for?" Baz quizzed, angrily.

"I work for British Intelligence and I need your help."

"So you are a female James Bond?"

Despite the sombre occasion, Lara couldn't help but smile. "I prefer wine to martinis. Now let's get serious. You have been caught with your pants down around your ankles and I need your help."

"With what?"

"You are involved in moving funds out of the country to support terrorism. Something which, if your government was made aware of your crime, would result in a very slow and painful death."

Baz was sweating despite the air conditioning. "What do you want?"

"I want to know everything. Your contacts in ISIS, who is contributing the funds. Everything."

"You bitch," he said succinctly. "What's to stop me just killing you. There is no evidence to support what you say."

"Nothing concrete perhaps but there is this." She took some photos and a computer stick from her bag. The photos showed him entering the apartment followed a short time later by her entering. He was easily distinguishable even though she was not. The photos had been taken by a colleague from the embassy.

"This means nothing," he said. "It doesn't prove anything."

"True, but if you listen to the audio file on the stick, you will hear everything that happened between us last time we were here. You will recall that you turned me on so much I kept calling out your name, asking you to fuck me and telling you how much I like what you were doing. If this was to fall into the wrong hands… Well I don't need to explain what would happen. You know better than me."

"I will simply kill myself and put an end to your sordid attempt at blackmail. Or even better, maybe I will kill you slowly first and then myself."

"That is not necessary." Lara was a good judge of character and didn't believe for one minute Baz was seriously contemplating ending his own life. It had been her judgement that Baz would fall for her charms and she had been proved correct. "We do not want to cause you distress. In fact, we want you to continue with your life as if nothing at all has changed. That is actually very important. We will do nothing to reveal our sources but your input will be invaluable to us, as you can imagine. We will even pay you for your information."

"You are evil! And if you know anything about me, you know I do not need more money."

"I am evil! I think that's a bit rich coming from someone helping to fund global terrorism. But I don't want to get into an argument about ideals.

There is one further incentive I can offer you."

"What is that?"

It was time for her to play her ace. She described what she could do for him.

"You give me a lot to think about."

"I need your agreement before I leave here. Otherwise, I won't be able to control what happens next. If you will not agree to help us immediately, my superiors will win favour with your government by revealing details of your treachery and infidelity. If that happens, I think we can assume by this time tomorrow you will be in a great deal of pain. You probably have first-hand experience of how effective certain of your colleagues are at extracting information and confessions."

Baz had gone white. He had seen his country's torturers at work. He knew what she said was true. No one ever resisted for very long. "We have already established you are a whore," he said. "Name your price to destroy this evidence and I will see it is deposited in a Swiss bank account before the morning."

"I am not for sale."

"A million dollars."

Lara was shocked by the size of the offer and the thought it could be in a bank account of her choice by morning. She could wake up rich. It was a little bit tempting. She could work the rest of her adult life and never expect to see a million dollars in her back account. Neither teaching or intelligence work paid very well.

"Not even for ten million dollars," she said, returning to reality. "Now what is your answer? Will you give us what we want?"

Baz went quiet for a moment before replying, "You know my answer." His shoulders sagged and he put his head in his hands. "You don't give me any choice. But I am only a very small cog in an irresistible movement that will not be stopped. You may win this small victory but you will lose the war."

"That remains to be seen." Lara knew she had to choose her words carefully and could not allow her true emotions to show. She despised Baz and a part of her almost wished him to refuse to help so he would get the summary justice the Saudi state would hand out. But she had a job to do and Baz offered huge potential for combatting terrorism by cutting of the finances that fuelled their war and identifying other contacts.

"You've made a wise decision," Lara continued. She took pen and paper from her bag. "Write down here details of your major contacts. I will question you further over the coming weeks and we will compile a detailed history of your actions and further contacts but this will be enough to keep my superiors happy for the time being. Do not lie or try to avoid telling me anything. This is not the chance for you to settle any personal scores by giving us false names. We have another person inside the organisation and we will be checking one set of information against the other. At the first sign of your dishonesty or withholding something we need to know, you will be signing your own death warrant."

CHAPTER FORTY THREE

Lara returned to her home to find a different atmosphere in the house. Everyone was eagerly anticipating leaving next morning and having lunch in Bahrain. Even Karim seemed happy to be leaving. The house had become claustrophobic and going anywhere seemed a good idea.

Lara went straight to the bathroom, took the papers Baz had filled with contact details from her bag and placed them in a plastic, waterproof bag, which she then taped to the inside of the pedestal that supported the washbasin. They would have to remain there until the next day when she could deliver them to her contact from the embassy. She had already called and in coded terms revealed she needed to make a drop. It was the first of many, she hoped.

She was in an exuberant and carefree mood. She knew her career would take a massive leap forward as a result of her becoming Baz's handler. He was potentially one of the most important assets in the war against terrorism. With his information she would quickly climb through the ranks. There would be jealousy from colleagues but they would have to treat her with kid gloves. She would be too important for any of them to piss off and risk her wrath.

She wanted to celebrate. As there was nothing alcoholic to drink in the house, she would celebrate the only other way she knew, by once again fucking Powell's brains out. She liked him and the sex was good. Actually, it was better than just good.

In a different world maybe they would have a chance of something real developing but she had not spent so many years trying to build a career, to throw it away for any man. Once he was gone she would again have to adjust to a life without any sex so she would have to make the best of this opportunity.

Returning to join the others she said, "We need to be ready to leave tomorrow morning at seven so Karim and Laila, I suggest after dinner you go straight to bed."

"Powell, can you help me in the kitchen, please."

Powell followed Lara to the kitchen and playfully smacked her on her bottom once they were out of sight of everyone else. "I think we should also get an early night but I'm not sure we're going to get much sleep."

"Then I better explain the plan while I can still concentrate. There will be two cars coming in the morning to collect us. You and Jenkins will be in the first with two of my colleagues from the embassy who genuinely want to get away for the weekend. They will have the necessary paperwork for themselves and two other colleagues from the embassy who are roughly your age and looks. This is only good for you if you are stopped before you reach the causeway. You can't use their ID to leave the country as they will then be unable later to explain why they are still here."

"What happens at the causeway?"

"Basically, you meet our contact, who takes your passports to an office, provides all the stamps you need, returns the passports and then you all drive across the causeway to Bahrain and freedom."

"Sounds like I'm going to owe a great number of people a large drink. Just as well I own a bar! What about the children?"

"The kids and I are going in the second car with another colleague. He's a local with a family and his children are of a similar age to Karim and Laila. We will be travelling as his family. I will wear a Niqab and the photos of the children are several years old so we shouldn't encounter any problems on the way. The contact at the border will give us the necessary stamps when we return without any children."

Powell hadn't considered the possibility of travelling separately from the children and it made him uncomfortable but the plan also made sense. In fact it was so good he was wondering how come Lara had been able to pull so many strings and get so much support. Perhaps she was rather more senior than he had been giving her credit for or maybe the British authorities were just keen to get them out of the country as soon as possible, to save the further risk of an embarrassing incident.

"I like your plan," Powell said. "Even if Jenkins and I have any problems, the children can still make it across. I called their mother earlier today and she is already on a flight. She'll be waiting for you."

Lara was slightly taken aback. "I didn't realise she would be flying to Bahrain."

"Try stopping her! British passport holders don't need an advance visa, you just buy one at the point of entry so there was no reason for her not to travel. And it will also be good for the children. They will want to see their mother as soon as possible."

"I guess that makes sense."

"As a parent, I understand her desperation to see her children after so long away. I would have done exactly the same."

"Let's hope we have no problems."

CHAPTER FORTY FOUR

Powell felt like he had only just fallen asleep when his alarm announced it was time to wake up. Lara had been true to her word and not allowed him much sleep, not that he had been an unwilling partner. She had frantically taken and given in equal measures of passion, leaving him completely satisfied. In fact he was more than satisfied, he was completely knackered in a way he hadn't been for many years.

Considering what lay ahead, he probably should have taken the athlete approach of no sex before a big event. In truth though, he would have gone without any sleep if she had wanted more. He would have done anything she asked of him, such was the attraction and desire he felt.

He was going to miss her when he returned to England and there was no realistic chance of them having an ongoing relationship. Typical of his luck in life with women or the lack of it, he had finally met someone he would like to get serious about and it looked like she would only get to play a fleeting role in his life story.

He made some coffee while he heard people start to move about upstairs. They all had small overnight bags, which they had mostly packed the previous night, to keep up the pretence of visiting Bahrain for just one night.

Powell was looking forward to a night in a five star hotel with Lara. They would be able to share a King size bed, have a bottle of wine and enjoy a bit of luxury. He would even allow her to be noisy as there would be no one upstairs to overhear them. In fact, he was going to damn well encourage it!

Jenkins was first downstairs, followed not long after by everyone else. No one felt like breakfast and the children were promised a McDonalds for lunch in Bahrain, which made them happy.

Powell took Karim aside and asked him directly, "Are you happy to be going back to England?"

"I've thought about what you said. You know, about father telling us our mother was dead. That was a terrible thing to do. He was always saying how important it is to tell the truth even if you fear the consequences. He was a hypocrite and though I do love him, I think it is right that we go see our mother. She must have been very worried about us."

"You sound like a very sensible young man. Your parents should be very proud of you. And I'm glad to see my offer to take you to see the mighty Arsenal had no influence on your decision."

"You are still going to take me though?"

"I certainly am. Do you think we could get your mother and sister to come?"

Karim looked doubtful. "Probably not but we can ask them."

Powell was relieved by Karim's change in attitude. Powell was confident he could be trusted not to say anything out of place.

The first car arrived to collect Powell and Jenkins. They had decided they would start ten minutes ahead of the others and communicate details of any checkpoints or other issues they encountered on the way. They had said goodbyes but were hoping to all be meeting up again in Bahrain in about five hours.

Ben and David were introduced as their travelling companions. They were sat in the front of the car with Powell and Jenkins in the back. Powell recognised their type. They were both about thirty with athletic builds, short hair styles and chiselled jaws.

"Whereabouts in England are you guys from?" Ben inquired.

"I'm from Swansea in Wales and proud of it," Jenkins replied good naturedly with a heavier than usual Welsh accent. "I believe England's that place next door we are going to be beating in the rugby world cup."

"Brighton," Powell answered simply. He was deep in thought and his mind elsewhere.

"A rugby fan eh?" David asked.

"I said I was Welsh didn't I?"

"I'll miss having a pint while I watch the games," Ben admitted.

"I'll be having quite a few I imagine, especially when we're celebrating victory after the game."

"I'll buy the first round once we reach Bahrain," David offered.

"Sounds good to me," Jenkins replied.

The journey was tedious. There was nothing to see outside the car windows except mile after mile of the same flat, barren landscape. They stopped at a petrol station to get some drinks and snacks. Powell stretched his legs and decided to call Lara.

"How's it going?" he asked.

"No problems so far. How about you?"

"Okay. Nothing out of the ordinary to report. We've about another two hours of driving before it gets interesting."

"I'm sure it will all be fine," Lara said. "You'll soon be back in England. I'm quite jealous."

"I promise to think of you each time I open a bottle of champagne back in my bar," Powell teased.

"Thanks for nothing. I'll be thinking of you when I'm in bed all by myself."

"But tonight we can sleep together in a decent sized bed and we can drink copious amounts of good quality champagne. Should be quite a night."

"Sounds like fun," Lara agreed.

"On that note, I think I'd better go. Say hello to the kids from me."

"I will. See you later."

CHAPTER FORTY FIVE

"We're there," Ben announced unnecessarily, as the queue of traffic was evidence enough they had arrived. "Let me do all the talking."

"My lips are sealed," Powell replied. He was more than happy to leave everything to Ben, who by all accounts had a proven track record of getting people across the causeway.

Powell's butterflies had started working overtime. He glanced out the windows at some of the other cars, just in case he could spot Lara and the children but there was no sign of them, which wasn't surprising as they were ten minutes away.

Ben surprised Powell by immediately driving into the services at the entrance to the causeway. He parked on the side not in front of a petrol pump. He dialled a number and said simply, "We're here."

They sat in the car for twenty minutes, Powell becoming ever more nervous. He said nothing, there was nothing to say. Within a short time they were either going to be hauled off to jail to endure his worst nightmare or they would be drinking beer in Bahrain.

The contrast in how they would potentially spend the evening could not be greater and the longer they waited in the car, the more Powell worried there was a problem. However, he was pleased to see Ben showed no signs of being agitated by the long wait. Powell had no way of knowing how far the man had to come from. Perhaps this was perfectly normal.

Finally a man walked towards their car. "This is him," Ben said, winding down his window and sitting upright.

"Hello," the man said, shaking hands with Ben through the window. "Follow me as usual." He glanced at the passengers in the back but said nothing further and then walked away.

The man looked like any other ordinary Saudi citizen, dressed in his white robes but to Powell he was far from ordinary. Powell's nerves were under better control now the contact had arrived and the confirmation they had done this before gave him some confidence.

A couple of minutes later the contact reappeared in his car, a top of the range BMW. Helping people across the border was obviously remunerative work.

Ben followed the contact back onto the bridge and remained directly behind him as the traffic slowly inched forward. "This first checkpoint is the easy one," he said. "It just ensures I own the car."

Powell hadn't realized there was more than one checkpoint. Eventually, it was their turn at the window and Ben handed across some documents. They sat in silence until after a minute, the documents were handed back and Ben was able to continue.

Powell breathed his first sigh of relief and smiled at Jenkins.

Ben pulled into the side of the road behind the BMW. He got out of the driver's seat and joined them in the back. Powell and Jenkins shuffled across to give him room. The contact walked form his car and took Ben's place in the driver's seat. Powell assumed events were about to get serious.

After a short distance, the contact took a left between a set of buildings in the center of the causeway all the way through to the opposite side of the bridge and began to drive against the flow of traffic coming from Bahrain, using a lane probably reserved for emergency traffic.

He stopped alongside another set of buildings about fifty meters from the last checkpoint coming from Bahrain. A security guard from the checkpoint walked towards the car and Powell held his breath. The driver wound down his window and spoke with the guard for a minute.

A box was handed over by the guard and passed to the back seat. Ben instructed Powell and Jenkins to put their passports inside the box. It was then returned to the guard, who walked slowly back to the checkpoint.

The time ticked by and Powell had never felt more nervous in his life. He had checked his watch for the hundredth time when the guard finally reappeared. He had only been gone ten minutes but it had felt three times as long. The guard walked back towards the car by himself. Surely, if there was a problem he would be accompanied by others wielding guns. The guard said something brief to the driver and handed back the passports.

The driver pulled away and took another small alleyway between the buildings to return to the other side of the bridge and back into the normal flow of traffic towards Bahrain.

Powell could see the final Saudi checkpoint up ahead and knew this was the one that mattered. The butterflies returned as their turn at the checkpoint arrived. They handed over the passports, which were only briefly inspected and then returned without problem.

As they left the checkpoint behind them and headed into Bahrain without problem, Powell had never felt so in need of a long, cold beer.

CHAPTER FORTY SIX

Ben, David and their contact had deposited them at the first pub on the way into the city centre. There had been no conversation during the remainder of the journey across the causeway, except for the contact to ask if Ben could drop him in the centre of town. Powell had sent a brief message to Lara saying they were in Bahrain.

Powell gave Ben his phone number and told them to call if they fancied meeting up later for a drink and made it very clear he would be paying for all the drinks. They watched Ben reclaim the driver's seat and head into the centre of town and then they hurried inside the bar.

The sense of relief Powell felt was huge. He stood at the bar with the biggest grin imaginable on his face as the barman handed them two pints of lager. They both downed about half without saying anything and then took the remainder of their beers and sat at a table in the corner.

"The others shouldn't be long now," Powell said.

"They'll be okay," Jenkins said reassuringly. "Their papers are in order and they will breeze through. It's tomorrow when Lara returns with Mister Fixit that they are doing the dodgy bit. And by then we will be on our way back to England."

Although he was feeling a huge surge of excitement, Powell knew he must reign in his exuberant mood until he received confirmation the children were safe. Angela Bennett would already have arrived at the Hilton but he didn't want to call her until the children had safely arrived.

After half an hour, Powell decided he couldn't wait any longer and called Lara. The call went straight to voicemail and he left a short message asking her to call back.

He was slightly worried but reasoned Lara had probably turned the phone off while they went through the Saudi checkpoints. He went to the bar and ordered two more beers. After a further thirty minutes of silence he called again with the same result.

"Shit," he swore. His good mood had rapidly evaporated. "They must have been held."

"Call Ben and see if he's heard anything," Jenkins suggested.

"I don't have his number. He said he'd call us later."

They both shared a concerned look.

"Who else can we call?" Jenkins asked.

"I'll try Martin Thwaite." Powell was relieved when Thwaite answered the phone.

"Have you heard from Lara by any chance?" Powell asked.

"Not today. Is everything all right?"

"Jenkins and I are in Bahrain but there's no sign of Lara or the children."

"Sorry, I can't help. I'll get her to call you if I hear from her."

"Thanks."

Powell tried Lara's number again and left a further message when it went to voicemail. He was now convinced there was a problem.

Powell's phone signalled an incoming message. He was relieved when he saw it was from Lara.

"What is it?" Jenkins queried, seeing the look on Powell's face.

Powell had read the message twice in disbelief. He passed his phone to Jenkins and took a large drink of his beer.

"Fuck," Jenkins swore after reading the message. "I don't believe it."

Neither did Powell. He took back his phone and reread the message:

Powell, sorry to do this to you but I've returned the children to their father. I really had no choice. You can work out the reason if you remember our previous conversations. I argued with my boss but he insisted. I felt I owed it to you to get you to safety. Return to Brighton and get on with your life. Lara.

"What does she mean about the previous conversations?" Jenkins inquired.

"The children's father is suspected of working with ISIS. I would hazard a guess she must have done a deal to give back the children in return for information."

"We're lucky she let us get out of the country alive," Jenkins said. "We know stuff that makes us a risk. Spooks don't normally let people walk around with what we know in our heads."

"I'm not sure she was being entirely altruistic. She wouldn't have wanted us to be taken by the Saudis. We could have done a deal with them based on what we know. She had to either kill us or get us out of the country."

I prefer to believe she just really liked us." Jenkins grinned then added, "Well she must have liked at least one of us."

Powell realised there was some truth in that statement. She would have been better served by tidying up all the loose ends but instead had helped them get to safety.

"It's my fault," Powell stated. "I fell for her pretty face and trusted her too easily. I shouldn't have let the kids out of my sight." He remembered how she made love the last time. It was as if it would be their last time ever, which of course she had known it would be.

"Don't be too hard on yourself. I would have fallen the same way given half a chance," Jenkins conceded.

"How the fuck am I going to tell Angela Bennett," Powell thought out loud.

CHAPTER FORTY SEVEN

Powell was deeply troubled he'd let down Angela Bennett but even worse was the feeling of having been played for an idiot by Lara. She'd waved her body at him and like a teenage virgin, he'd allowed her to take over his operation for her own ends.

Powell was sat in the bar of the Hilton with Angela Bennett. Jenkins was in his room as Powell felt it befell him to update his employer. He recounted everything that had happened from the time they arrived in Saudi and she had been very understanding. Inside, she was heartbroken but she knew they had done everything possible to rescue the children and said so more than once.

She was particularly shocked to hear about Baz's links to ISIS and his role in helping fund terrorism. Powell also explained that Baz wasn't just a clerk handling visa applications but someone quite senior in the Saudi intelligence service.

"Are you saying he is a spy?" Angela asked disbelievingly.

"Yes," Powell confirmed.

"Even when he was in England, living with me?"

"Yes."

"You've all had too much sun."

"I promise you it's true. Baz was and is what we call a spook. While he was in England he was no doubt an important member of the Saudi intelligence community."

"I bet he wasn't playing golf half the time," she said. "No one plays that much golf."

"You may well be right. Golf makes a good excuse for meeting people."

"And you are equally sure he is part of ISIS?"

"MI6 is convinced."

"Well that explains a great deal."

"What do you mean?"

"Well I understand now why the government would find his information more important than the lives of two small children.

Powell was surprised at how she claimed to understand her government's actions, even if she didn't condone them. She was an astute woman and not naïve about the ways of the world.

Most mothers he knew would simply have broken down in the face of impossible odds but she was still determined to get her children back. She was going to return to England to continue campaigning. She had a meeting arranged with her local member of parliament and she now had more ammunition for pushing the government into helping her cause.

Powell was worried she might think she could use what he had told her about Baz and ISIS to blackmail the government into helping her recover her children. He warned her against ever saying anything in public or to a newspaper. She seemed to grasp the implications of what he was saying.

Baz was such a significant asset, Powell had no doubt MI6 would go to any odds to protect him and that might include silencing Angela Bennett. Hell, even he and Jenkins weren't necessarily safe. He didn't want to be suffering any unlucky accidents in the near future. The fact they had both worked for the Security Services, albeit Jenkins in an unofficial capacity, would hopefully convince the powers to be that they could be trusted to keep their mouths shut. Brian would be able to put in a good word for them, probably already had done.

Powell could recall from his time in the Security Services when decisions were made, which would inevitably lead to someone innocent being killed but they deemed it necessary for the greater good. He could imagine the spooks sitting around a table debating whether they should let them live or die. He wondered how he had ever been party to some of the things that took place in the old days.

If Angela's meeting with her member of parliament was a dead end then she had decided her next step would be to look for a job in Saudi, maybe teaching English at a language school. She would never give up on getting back her children. Powell was sure that if Angela did end up in Saudi, she would be paying Lara a visit. He would like to be a fly on the wall at that meeting.

Before going to bed, Angela wished him well in the future and thanked him again for what he and Jenkins had done. At least her children now knew she wasn't dead and was desperately trying to get them home. Baz would be dealing with some very difficult questions from Karim and Laila. Perhaps they would be able to shame him into doing the right thing and granting her some form of access.

"This stinks," Jenkins said as he joined Powell in the bar.

They had decided to move on from beer to shorts so both of them were now drinking whisky. In Powell's case with ice and ginger ale. Jenkins had it with just a little water added.

"I can't just go home and pretend none of this ever happened," Powell said, looking down at his drink and nodding his head from side to side.

"We have no choice."

"You don't understand. If I don't bring those children home, Bella's death was for nothing."

"How's that?"

"If I can achieve some positive outcomes, helping people in need, then Bella didn't die for nothing. If she was still alive, I'd be back at my bar living life as I had for the last twenty years but because of her death, I'm in Bahrain trying to right a serious wrong. Some good can come out of her death and that makes it just a little bit more bearable."

"There'll be other opportunities, it's not as if there is any shortage of things needing putting right in the world."

Powell knew what he needed to do but this time he would work alone. "I'm going back," he said with conviction.

"It's madness. You'll never get to the kids again."

"Not necessarily true. They definitely won't be expecting me to try again. Lara will have told Baz I am safely out of the country and on my way back to England."

"What's with this 'me'?"

"You're going home. It is madness and I don't want you getting further involved."

"Wait a minute," Jenkins interrupted. "Even as a team it's proved difficult. You need my help."

"It's too risky. I'm very grateful for what you've done so far but I'm ending your contract. If I need your help, I know how to get hold of you."

"You're serious aren't you?"

"Very. In the morning I'm going back over the causeway alone. My passport is in order and I'm going to return from a weekend away like so many others."

Powell would never be able to live with himself if he took Jenkins with him and they ended up getting caught. It was okay for him to act foolishly but Jenkins had more life left to live. He'd mentioned that one day he would like to have children like Karim and Laila. He couldn't do that from inside a Saudi jail.

"Have you told Angela?" Jenkins asked.

"No, I don't want her to know. I don't want to raise her hopes anymore. She's been through enough. If you see her in the morning tell her I already left for England."

"How you going to get out next time? Of course, you could always ask Lara for help, I guess," Jenkins said sarcastically. "Even if you can get the kids to go with you again, you now know how difficult it is to get out the damned country."

"I'll worry about that tomorrow. Tonight I just want a few drinks."

CHAPTER FORTY EIGHT

Powell slept in until late morning and was definitely nursing a bit of a hangover when he ordered brunch in the smaller of the hotel's restaurants, which stayed open all day. Feeling better, he hired a car and paid the necessary insurance to be able to take it into Saudi. He chose a Toyota Land Cruiser, which was just about the biggest vehicle he'd ever driven but he quickly found it wasn't short of acceleration or speed.

The reverse journey over the causeway went without incident. Powell felt quite relaxed because with the children returned to their father, he was fairly certain he was no longer being hunted. Certainly, no one could expect him to be re-entering the country. He was using the passport in the name of Smith, which was a risk but less of one than using his own name because it now had the correct stamps.

He knew most people enjoyed the weekend to the full in Bahrain and didn't return until the evening so he intentionally set off at two o'clock to miss the worst of the traffic. He sailed through the checkpoints and was soon speeding towards Riyadh.

The journey gave him plenty of time to think and he decided he needed to strike quickly, while they expected him to be licking his wounds and on the way back to England. He hoped Baz hadn't decided to take the children to live somewhere else but that seemed unlikely. His work probably required him to be in Riyadh and the kids were enrolled at school.

If Lara was pumping him for information then she wouldn't agree to his rushing off anywhere but returning his kids didn't seem enough reason to justify his turning on ISIS. Perhaps she had discovered evidence of his involvement with ISIS and was blackmailing him. That was more likely.

Then it hit him like a thunderbolt. Could she have snared Baz with her body like she had him? After all, he had easily fallen for her charms. He had foolishly thought he was attractive enough for her to be desperate to sleep with him the very first evening they had spent in her house. What was he thinking? She was a beautiful woman and there must have been better options available to her.

Where had she gone the second night they spent in the house? She had returned late, having lost her appetite for sex. He remembered it clearly now. She had said she had a meeting to discuss how to get them out of Saudi. He swore out loud at his stupidity and his gullibility.

The more he thought about it, the more he believed Lara had played both him and Baz like some sort of Mata Hari. As that thought developed so did the answer to how he would persuade Lara to help him get the children out of the country.

He drove straight to the centre of the city and spent a couple of hours searching the shops for what he wanted. Eventually a helpful assistant in one shop directed him to a large shop on the edge of town, which sold the one important thing outstanding and without which his plan could not succeed.

He drove to the compound and slowed at the entrance to speak with the guard.

"Hello," he said, cheerfully. "Me again. I'm visiting Martin Thwaite."

The guard checked the list on his clipboard. He wrote down the car's registration and then waved him through.

Powell drove towards Thwaite's house but once out of sight of the gate he changed direction and parked a few houses from where Lara lived.

As he approached the house he was pleased to see Lara's lights were on, which suggested she was home. It was nine at night and he would have been surprised not to find her home.

He walked confidently to the front door and knocked. He turned his back on the spyhole, hoping Lara would open the door despite not being able to see who was outside.

She obviously felt secure in her home because she quickly opened the door. He turned to face her and enjoyed the look of shock on her face.

"Don't worry," Powell said pleasantly. "I'm not here to cause any trouble. I was in the process of booking a flight back to my empty house in Brighton and started thinking about our time together and well... here I am!"

"Are you mad?" Lara asked but she forced a smile.

"Look, I haven't been with anyone for a very long time and it's not easy to walk away from something as good as we shared. Even if it was just sex for you, it was bloody good sex. At least I thought so."

"Yes, it was pretty good," she admitted, grinning. "You better come in."

"I understand why your boss made the call he did and I can't blame you for his decisions," Powell said, as they walked through to the lounge. "Baz is obviously a very big fish. I'm not naïve and had to make my share of tough decisions back in my days in the Security Services."

"Thanks. I've been feeling bad about what I did but I really didn't have a choice… Not if I wanted to keep my job."

"You could have just handed me over to the authorities but instead you got me out of the country. I owe you big time for that and rest assured neither Jenkins or I would ever say a word about what we know."

"Where is Jenkins?" Lara inquired.

"He went back to England this morning with Angela Bennett. But enough of them. I just wanted to see you one more time. See if perhaps there is any future for us."

Lara smiled and seemed to relax for the first time since he'd entered the house. She moved towards him and reached up and touched her lips lightly against his before pulling them away in a tease. She did it again and again until finally she kissed him passionately. When she was finished she said, "Probably no long term future but we don't have to worry about that tonight."

"Can I have a shower?" Powell asked.

"Of course. You know the way."

"Give me five minutes and you might like to join me."

"I'll be right up."

Powell hurried to the shower and undressed. He carefully placed his clothes over the towel rail.

Within a few minutes he was joined by Lara.

"You realise this is actually the first time I've seen you naked," Powell said.

"You suffering from early Alzheimer's or something?"

"It's true. We've only made love on your sofa in the dark."

"And what do you think?" She put her hands on her hips and adopted a provocative pose.

"Stunning."

"You're not so bad yourself," she said, as she lifted her mouth upwards to invite further kisses.

Unlike the previous occasions he was more dominant as he made love to her, pushing her to her knees to suck on him, while the shower cascaded over her head. Then he turned her around and banged her hard against the shower door. The sex was steamy but so was the shower cubicle and didn't really suit his purpose.

"Let's go to the bedroom," he suggested, pulling her out of the shower. He took a towel and briefly dried her body. "I'll be with you in a minute."

"You better be."

He towelled himself dry, then took hold of his clothes and went through to the bedroom. She had lain down naked on top of the bed. He placed his clothes neatly on top of a chest of drawers.

"Hurry up," Lara encouraged.

He turned to face her. "What would you like to do now?" he teased. His cock was standing upright and there was no doubt where her gaze was fixed.

"I'd like to try and swallow all of that."

"You're a very naughty woman," he chided jokingly. "Single women aren't supposed to behave like this in Saudi."

"Maybe but I am feeling very horny."

"Actually, you may have noticed, I am as well."

CHAPTER FORTY NINE

Powell lay on the bed exhausted by the night's sex. The fact they had a large double bed and an empty house had encouraged Lara to get rid of all her inhibitions, if she ever had any, and she had noisily enjoyed Powell in a variety of positions. He certainly wasn't complaining, as it had been physically satisfying if not emotionally. He was also certain it had achieved its purpose but he wouldn't be able to check properly until later.

"I didn't want to leave on bad terms," Powell said, as Lara returned to bed with two mugs of coffee. "If I hadn't done this, I'd never have seen you again. It would have been an unsatisfactory way to end whatever it was we had. Of course, if you now tell me it was fun but that was all it was, then I really do understand. I'm not going to start stalking you or anything! You have my phone number and next time you are in England, I hope you call me and visit me in Brighton so we can have some more fun."

"Well it was definitely fun! Was that all it was, I'm not sure. It doesn't seem practical to develop a meaningful relationship so far apart. But I'll definitely look you up next time I'm back in the UK."

"That's good enough for me. I need a shower and then I'll be out of your hair. I'm going to drive back to Bahrain as I have to return the hire car. If you ever fancy a weekend together in Bahrain, give me a call."

"That sounds a wonderful idea. Let's go share a shower and I'm going to suck out the last bit of spunk left in your balls as a going away present."

Powell was happy as he walked back to his car. Lara was both physically beautiful and a great lover, which didn't always go hand in hand. She had made it easy for him to get what he needed. She had snatched at the chance of some momentary pleasure and now would have to pay the price for her actions.

He had some degree of sympathy for how she had behaved regarding the children. She did a difficult job, which he knew from his own experience make it impossible to lead a normal life. While he had been running a bar in Brighton she had been fighting global terrorism in the Middle East. The two responsibilities didn't really compare. Lara and her kind were needed so those back home in their beds in England could sleep safely.

She had been trained to use those around her as nothing more than assets to achieve her operational aim. She would be entirely focused on the job in hand but she was still human and had grabbed at the chance of a bit of normality by having sex with him.

In normal circumstances, he would respect Lara for the job she did but this had become personal. Funny how something you are willing to accept is okay when it happens to other people, becomes something quite different when it becomes personal. Her dark world had touched upon his life. The decision made by her boss was not affecting some faceless person, it was two children he had grown to like. They were not his own children but they were Angela Bennett's children and their family deserved to be reunited. He wondered what reaction he would get next time he appeared on Lara's doorstep. He couldn't imagine her being very welcoming.

He drove straight to the school gates and arrived in time to see the children arrive. There was one significant change in their routine. As well as the driver, another man was sat in the front passenger seat. Was he just being dropped somewhere or was he a permanent new addition to the routine, in the form of a bodyguard?

The children had walked slowly into school and didn't hurry with the enthusiasm he had seen displayed previously. Powell interpreted it as a sign they weren't happy to be back in their old routine. Powell was relieved Baz had insisted on them going straight back to school and making his job easier. They would have quite a story to tell their friends.

Powell had to do a number of things to prepare for the afternoon when he planned to take the children. He drove towards the airport hotel and returned by taxi. Preparations completed, he found he still had a couple of hours free, which he spent at the shopping mall, where he purchased a laptop and drank copious amounts of coffee. He emailed copies of his files to Brian with instructions and to his personal account at the bar.

He thought about Lara and Afina, and how different they both were. He had used Lara last night but felt vindicated by the fact she had previously used him. He didn't hate her for what she'd done but he also knew he could never have a relationship with her because he could never fully trust her. That was the fault of the job she did.

Afina was quite different. Powell knew he could implicitly trust Afina. She would not lie to him or use him for her personal benefit. There was only one of them he could ever see himself having a proper relationship with but every time he thought about the longer term and Afina, his doubts resurfaced.

Finally it was time to leave and he took a taxi back to the end of the road where the school was located. The Range Rover arrived before the kids emerged, complete with its additional passenger and damage to one wing. He wasn't entirely surprised by the presence of further security but it was definitely unwelcome. There was a strong likelihood the guard would be armed, which certainly added an extra dimension to what he was planning. At least neither men in the Range Rover knew who he was, which was a small mercy.

CHAPTER FIFTY

Powell knew the direction from which the Range Rover would arrive and where it would park. He had positioned himself fifty metres down the road behind the car. He walked briskly along the pavement towards the vehicle, carrying the small bag he had purchased earlier, which contained everything he needed. One hand was inside the bag, gripping the heavy wrench. As he came level with the rear doors, he was grateful to see they were already unlocked.

Without breaking stride, he dropped the bag to the floor and pulled open the passenger door. He delivered a heavy blow with the wrench to the side of the head of the man sat inside. The guard literally never knew what hit him and the effect was immediate as he was knocked unconscious.

The driver was quickly grappling with his own door handle, seemingly desperate to escape. Powell reached across and grabbed hold of his arm, glad the driver's first instinct had been to run away not drive away.

"Stay where you are," Powell shouted, raising the wrench in a threatening manner.

The driver cowered in his seat with his hands up to ward off any blow.

Powell was already removing the weapon from the guard's shoulder holster with his free hand. He waved it at the driver. "Sit quietly and you won't be hurt," he commanded.

The driver did as instructed, allowing Powell the chance to pick up his bag from the floor and jump in the back seat. None of the mothers hanging around the school gates was showing any sign of having noticed what had happened. Fortunately, they were all facing the gates, waiting for their little ones to emerge.

"When the children come out just behave normally. I don't want any trouble."

"For a man who doesn't want trouble you have a very strange way of showing it," the driver replied.

The guard had only been stunned and was now alert to the presence of Powell on the back seat.

"Do you speak English?" Powell asked the guard. Receiving no response, he turned to the driver and demanded, "Please translate for me."

"There is no need, he understands perfectly."

Powell prodded the guard sharply in the neck with the barrel of the gun. "I am here for the children. I need your driver but I don't need you. Therefore I suggest you don't play games with me. Just keep very still, say nothing and you will get to see the sun come up tomorrow."

The children were emerging from the school and Powell spotted Karim and Laila. They walked towards the car and due to the tinted windows were not aware of Powell's presence until Karim opened the door and started to climb inside.

"Get in," Powell instructed, seeing a momentary uncertainty on Karim's part. He was thankful they did as asked because if they had turned around and run away he would have been in a right mess.

"Time to go," he said to the driver. "Head for the airport."

"Are we flying to meet mummy?" Laila asked excitedly.

"Yes we are and this time no one is going to stop us."

Powell noticed Karim had a black eye and bruising to his cheek. "What happened to you?" he quizzed.

"Daddy hit him," Laila replied. "He blamed Karim for letting you take us away."

"I'm sorry," Powell apologised. "That wasn't fair of your father. It wasn't your fault"

"It doesn't hurt," Karim answered.

They drove for thirty minutes and then Powell directed the driver into the hotel car par. He showed him where to park in a quiet corner.

"Give me the keys," Powell said, once again pushing his gun into the driver's back, who handed them over.

Powell opened his bag and took out a pair of handcuffs. "Put your hands behind your back," he instructed the guard, with a prod from the gun to remind him not to argue. Powell closed the handcuffs over the guard's wrists.

He took out a further pair and told the driver to cuff his right hand to the steering wheel. He took out a third pair and cuffed the driver's left hand to the chain between the guard's cuffs. The man in the shop had looked at him as if he had a whole harem at home when he asked for three pairs.

He took the tape from his bag and wrapped it around their mouths so they wouldn't be able to shout for help. Next, he took the rope from his bag and secured both of them to the backs of their chairs sufficiently to stop them being able to lean forward onto the car horn. Finally he tied their legs together.

Powell surveyed his work. They would be uncomfortable but they were alive. There was a time when he would have simply settled for putting a bullet in each of them but that was the old Powell.

The tinted windows would make it difficult for anyone casually passing to spot what had happened inside the vehicle and the two occupants were not going to be able to easily attract attention.

"Okay, it's time to go," Powell announced to the children. "We have a flight to catch."

He led the way out of sight of the Range Rover to where he had left his Toyota earlier that morning. The children sat in the back and Powell accelerated away back towards town.

CHAPTER FIFTY ONE

As Powell reached the compound gates, he wound down his window and half leaned out, smiling at the guard who approached.

"Me again," he said. "Visiting the Thwaites."

The guard didn't even bother to record their entry and just waved them through.

Powell drove straight to Lara's home, hoping she wouldn't have any meetings to delay her arrival home from school.

"Stay in the car, while I check Lara is at home."

Karim looked anxious. "It was she who returned us to our father."

Powell realised Karim would not welcome another beating from his father. "It's okay," he assured them both. "You won't be going anywhere without me this time."

Powell walked up to the front door and knocked. He heard the footsteps on the other side of the door and knew he was being viewed through the spyhole. After a minute the door was opened, rather grudgingly he suspected, but she wouldn't want to draw attention to him stood on her doorstep for too long. She also would know he wasn't just going to go away.

"Yet another surprise visit," Lara said. "Are the kids in the car?"

"You know?"

"Baz called me demanding to know how to find you. I told him I had no idea, which was the truth."

"I need your help one last time."

"Not a chance in a million. He's already threatening to renege on our deal. I suppose I should have known when you came back it wasn't just because of me."

"I have something I want to show you. If you ask me to leave afterwards then I swear I will. I just need ten minutes of your time."

Lara unblocked the doorway as her answer and went back inside. Powell waved to the children to join him.

"Go in the kitchen and help yourselves to a drink," Powell suggested.

"Lara and I need some time alone."

The children obeyed without saying anything to Lara. Not really surprisingly, there was no greeting, not even a brief hello.

"I need you to get Ben to drive us through the causeway one more time," Powell said firmly. "Then we will be out of your hair for ever."

"I already told you 'no'. What did you want to show me? Your ten minutes is counting down."

"Did you see the bruise on Karim's face. That was from his father, who blamed him for being taken by us. If he ends up back with Baz again, there is no telling what he will do."

"That is hardly my problem. It's on your conscience not mine. Is that all you wanted to show me? Did you really expect a bruise to make me change my mind?"

Powell had thought there was a small chance Lara wouldn't need any more coercion and it had been worth a try. He took the USB stick from his pocket. "If you won't offer to help voluntarily then you should look at this."

She took hold of it like it was a hot coal. She placed it in her laptop, which was on a small table in the corner of the room.

Powell couldn't see the video playing but could tell from the sounds that she was watching them having sex the previous night.

After a minute she stopped the file and turned back towards him. "That's pretty tacky of you," she admonished. "What is it? A souvenir of your time in Saudi?"

"I wish it hadn't been necessary."

"How did you film it?"

"The wonders of modern technology. An amazing small camera in my belt."

"I thought at the time it was a bit odd how you took such care tidying your clothes before jumping into bed. You were positioning the camera."

"I've sent copies to various people, who will ensure they are published all over the internet, if you don't help me. A copy will also be sent to the Mutaween. If you were lucky you might get away with an enormous number of lashes and a prison sentence but I think it more likely they would want to make an example of you."

"You wouldn't do that to me. You're bluffing," Lara stated but without conviction.

"I don't play poker because I am rubbish at bluffing. You used me, which I could tolerate but you used two young children, who deserved better so please trust me when I say, I am not bluffing."

"Even if I wanted to help you I can't. My boss would never allow it a second time."

"Your boss is not going to burn all your good work with Baz for the lack of having your people drive me out of the country."

"I don't know if our contact is even working."

"Then you better find out quickly. We need to leave tonight or tomorrow morning at the latest. We are going to need visa stamps for the kids, which show they entered yesterday with me."

"My boss won't like this. He might decide the best answer is simply to get rid of you once and for all."

"Are you really trying to threaten me? I have personally nothing to lose. As you are aware, I have no important other and no children. My sole focus in life is getting those children back to their mother. I won't allow anything or anyone to get in my way. Not even a beautiful woman who I was developing strong feelings for and would have liked to stay in touch with in the future. And my friends are not the sort of people who can be intimidated. They will publish for sure if something happens to me."

CHAPTER FIFTY TWO

The timetable was driven by the fact the contact at the causeway was working the day shift. The plan was to set off from Lara's at six in the morning and arrive at the causeway about ten thirty. Unlike the previous trip, if they were subject to a random stop at any checkpoint, they would be in trouble as the children's papers were not in order. It was a risk Powell was prepared to take. He had to get out of the country as soon as possible.

Powell had barely slept and he certainly wasn't surprised that Lara didn't join him in his bed. It seemed even she had limits on when and with whom she took her pleasures. He woke the children at six and offered breakfast but neither of the children were hungry. Despite their young age they seemed to understand the seriousness of what lay ahead. Karim, in particular, had reason to fear being returned to his father.

"I have some good news," Lara anounced, joining him in the kitchen. "They located the car at three this morning. Given the close proximity to the airport and the fact both the driver and guard were convinced you were catching a plane, the authorities believe you have already escaped the country."

"Good news indeed but I'm not counting my chickens."

"Speaking of cars, what am I supposed to do with your hire car?"

"I'm sure you can work something out. I paid for four days."

"I'm sure I can."

Powell had a coffee and stayed in the kitchen waiting for Ben to arrive while Lara remained in the lounge. They had nothing further to say to each other.

When Ben did arrive, Powell sent the children out to the car so he could speak to Lara.

"Thanks for your help," Powell said, sincerely.

"I didn't have much choice."

"In the same way you didn't give the children any choice when you decided they had to go back to their father."

"Just promise me you will destroy all copies of the video as soon as you are back in England."

"I promise and I really am sorry it was necessary."

"I hope not to be seeing you again, Powell."

He couldn't find the words to make things better between them so he said nothing and headed for the car.

Ben drove within the speed limit and the journey was uneventful. As they approached the causeway, Powell was even more nervous than the last time. This really was the last chance saloon. Ben parked in the same services area and phoned his contact.

Powell had a feeling of déjà vu as they waited. He was pleased to see Ben looked relaxed. This was something he had done many times before without any problems. Ben had a diplomatic passport though and the worst he faced was being thrown out of the country.

They had to wait only ten minutes for the man who held their lives in his hands to arrive. He went through the same routine as the last time and seemed completely at ease with the presence of the children.

Powell remained alert for any signs of danger but there were none. At least no more than the last time they made the trip. A single guard collected their passports and they were returned after ten minutes with the necessary stamps.

As they approached the last checkpoint he glanced behind and smiled at the children, who were sitting very quietly. He handed over the passports to the guard and they were returned within a minute. Powell could barely believe everything had gone so smoothly as they accelerated away towards Bahrain and safety. Thank goodness the idea of two men travelling with two young children and no mother didn't seem strange to a Saudi. He was sure there would be far more questions asked in England.

Ben dropped them at the Hilton where Powell had reserved two rooms once they were physically across the Bahrain border. He walked into the hotel reception, casting his eyes around for signs of danger until he reminded himself there was no reason to feel threatened. They took the lifts to the third floor and Powell suggested the children join him in his room for a few minutes. He was then going to take them for the burgers and milk shakes they were craving.

Powell phoned Angela Bennett.

"Hello Powell, how are you?"

"Never felt better. I'm in Bahrain again and I have somebody who wants to speak to you." He handed the phone to Karim.

"Hello Mum," Karim said.

Powell heard the scream of pleasure from the other end of the phone. It was the best feeling he had experienced in a very long time.

CHAPTER FIFTY THREE

Powell arrived back in England exhausted by the events of the previous few weeks. The flight arrived at six in the morning and the children had slept the whole way but despite being worn out, Powell had slept only fitfully although he wasn't entirely sure why. Perhaps there was still too much adrenaline circulating in his body.

Angela Bennett was at Heathrow to meet her children and he was surprised to find Jenkins also waiting in arrivals. Watching the children run into their mother's arms had been as rewarding as he had expected. Jenkins explained he had come to see the children as he had never had the chance to say a proper goodbye to them in Saudi.

"I can never repay you for this," Angela said. "When I think what you risked for the three of us…" She dabbed at the corner of her eye.

"No tears," Powell urged. "This is a day for big smiles not tears."

"Thank you," she said for the hundredth time. "I need to get the children home now but when we are settled, I hope you are both going to come and pay us a visit in London."

"It will be my pleasure," Powell assured her. "Karim and Laila are very special."

"Count me in," Jenkins confirmed. "Sorry about Laila's hair by the way. I'm not exactly a trained hairdresser."

"It will grow back and thanks to both of you, I will get to see it grow."

Powell and Jenkins walked the family to their car and both received big hugs from Laila and a firm handshake from Karim.

"Take care of your mother and sister," Powell said to Karim. "You are the man of the house now."

"Remember about taking me to Arsenal," he replied.

"Don't worry, soon as I get home I'm going to check the fixtures. I'll speak with your mother to see if the girls want to come."

Karim jumped in the back of the car and the family drove away with everyone furiously waving goodbye out of the windows.

"You did a great thing there," Jenkins said. "I'm proud to have played a small part."

"Don't be daft. You played a massive part. It does make me feel good, seeing them back together. I know Bella would be very proud of what we achieved."

"I'm sure she would be… Right, I'll drive you back home now. It's a rather boring Volvo, not a fancy car like we've been used to driving in Saudi but it's never let me down."

"I'll only let you drive me if you're going to stay the night and help me celebrate."

"That was the plan."

Jenkins drove the hour and a quarter to Brighton while Powell explained how he had managed to get the children out of the country.

"I took your advice," Powell said. "I enlisted Lara's help again."

Jenkins looked at him strangely. "You mean Lara helped you? Why did she do that?"

"Well she wasn't keen at first but I can be very persuasive at times."

"You're not telling me something."

"And that is the way it will remain."

"I can see I'm going to have to get you very drunk to hear the whole story."

"You can try."

They arrived in Brighton at just after nine and parked on a meter, which meant they had a two minute walk to the bar. It had started raining lightly.

They stepped out of the car and just stood enjoying the sensation of the rain on them for a few seconds.

"I've been looking forward to some rain for weeks," Powell said.

"People will think we're mad standing here like this," Jenkins replied.

"Who cares."

As they arrived at the bar it had just opened to serve breakfast. They walked inside and Powell immediately noticed the newly painted wall.

"Powell!" Afina exclaimed and ran excitedly towards him.

"Hi Afina," he replied, as he was enveloped in a bear hug. "It's good to see you."

She stepped back and appraised him. "You look good. A suntan suits you."

"Thank you. It's good to be home. You remember Jenkins."

"Hello again," Afina said, turning to Jenkins, ignoring his outstretched hand and giving him a kiss on each cheek.

"That was worth the visit alone," Jenkins smiled. "But Powell has been telling me this bar makes the best breakfast in Brighton."

"What would you like?"

"The full works for both of us and two Lattes, please," Powell answered. "By the way, what happened to the wall?"

"I'll tell you about that later. Let me go organise the food first."

Powell had phoned Afina the previous evening, to let her know the operation had been successful and he was on his way home. Afina had seemed very happy at the news and Powell just thought she was looking forward to seeing him but he did wonder if she was relieved as much as happy. Had running the bar proved to be a bit more difficult than she had expected? He certainly hadn't found it easy in his early days as a novice bar owner.

Powell led the way to a table, accepting greetings from a couple of staff on the way. Afina brought their Lattes plus one for herself and pulled up a chair.

"What was Saudi like?" Afina asked.

"Hot," Jenkins replied succinctly.

"Not somewhere I want to go again," Powell added. "Not that I would be very welcome."

"Well I'm very glad to see you."

"What's been happening here?" Powell queried, becoming a little concerned. "What happened to the wall?"

CHAPTER FIFTY FOUR

Powell listened intently to Afina's retelling of events with growing horror. He thought he was rid of all his problems and had been planning to take a much needed holiday. Not probably a trip to anywhere hot, he'd had enough sun to last for a long time but a few days in the Lake District appealed, with plenty of long walks and great scenery. Everything he had missed while in Saudi.

"I spoke to Brian and he told me to do nothing until you got back," Afina explained. "He said you would know what to do."

"We could always just pay this Gheorghe a visit," Jenkins suggested. "And help him to see the error of his ways."

"I doubt we can intimidate him," Powell replied.

"Then perhaps a more permanent solution is needed," Jenkins suggested.

"I really appreciate you wanting to help but this is my problem," Powell stressed.

"Look, you didn't let me go back into Saudi with you but I'm sure as hell going to help you resolve this problem and I don't want to hear any arguments."

Powell realised he would need help if he was to deal with Gheorghe and also keep Afina, and the bar for that matter, safe.

"Okay, I surrender," Powell joked, raising his hands. "We need to act fast before they do any more damage to the bar and we can't just commit murder so... Any suggestions?"

"Mara has offered her help," Afina said. "Her uncle is expecting her to start working for him quite soon."

"Is she really going to return to her old way of life?" Powell asked, shocked.

"She doesn't feel she has any choice. I understand that feeling of being trapped." Afina was remembering when she returned to work as a prostitute when her family was threatened.

"I'm tired and not thinking clearly," Powell said. "Let's eat and then we can decide what action we take."

He had believed that with Dimitry's death there would no longer be any threat from Romania. He certainly hadn't expected to return from a difficult time in Saudi to what he was now facing.

Conversation over breakfast consisted mainly of Powell and Jenkins answering questions from Afina about their time in Saudi.

"Afina, tell Mara to let Gheorghe know I am back and planning to have a party on Friday night to celebrate my return. That gives us three days to prepare."

"You have a plan?" Jenkins asked.

"More an idea than a plan. We need to work on the detail."

"Life's certainly never boring around you," Jenkins joked.

"Once Mara tells Gheorghe you are back, your life is in danger," Afina warned.

"I think it's this Gheorghe who should be more worried," Jenkins suggested. "I've seen Powell at work and if he has a plan, nothing gets in his way."

Powell spent a large part of the remainder of the day on the phone. He had a long call with Angela Bennett, checking the children were okay and then discussing whether she should be concerned about Baz making any attempt to recover the children. Powell found it difficult to say with any certainty how Baz would react to the loss of his children.

Baz was a very wealthy and devious man. Apart from the pain any father would feel in his position, his pride would be hurt and Powell thought that might make him act rashly. He decided to call Lara and point out it was in both their interests that she had a word with Baz and warn him off doing anything stupid.

Once she had dealt with the shock of hearing his voice, she had agreed. She didn't want to see him travelling to England and getting himself arrested for child abduction. Powell didn't know exactly what she was blackmailing him with but had a good idea and took some wicked pleasure from pointing out she had him by the balls, whether it was literally true or not.

Powell had a long call with Brian and invited him to the upcoming party. He then made various other calls, including his mother and mother-in-law, who he hadn't spoken to for far too long.

Jenkins was going to kip down in the office rather than stay in a hotel to provide added security. They had dinner together and enjoyed a few long cold beers.

"Beer in the future will always taste the better for my dry experiences in Saudi," Jenkins said.

"I agree with that sentiment," Powell replied, raising his bottle and touching Jenkins bottle in a toast. "Here's to many more."

Afina was serving their table and after bringing further beers, Jenkins said, "I like Afina. She seems very capable as well as beautiful. Are you two…"

"No we're not," Powell stressed.

"Okay, just asking. And while we're on the subject…"

"What subject?"

"Dating. How is it you seem to do so well with the women when I'm younger and so much better looking."

"I'm actually crap with women and until recently I hadn't been on a date for more years than I can remember."

"I have to say that Lara was very beautiful… and noisy!" Jenkins burst into laughter.

"Don't know what you mean," Powell answered with a broad smile.

After dinner Powell took Afina aside and they shared a bottle of wine. He talked through his general idea for the Friday party.

"It's dangerous," Afina said. "Can't you talk to Gheorghe and try and make him see sense? Otherwise someone could be hurt or even killed."

"He sounds very similar to Dimitry and Victor. Would you have been able to make them see sense? I don't think so."

"But we should try. I will go speak with him. Mara can organise it."

"Don't go anywhere. I'll arrange to meet him and see if I can persuade him to go back home."

"Thank you, Powell. I missed you while you were away."

"I'm sorry I didn't call more but it was difficult."

"I understand. I think what you did was amazing."

"You deserve some time off. Why don't you take tomorrow off and go out with your friends."

"I can't leave you at a time like this."

"You need to have some fun with people your own age."

"I enjoy my work."

"All work and no play isn't healthy. You're young and beautiful. There are young men who would love to take you out."

"Such as who?"

"Luke for example. I know he likes you."

"I don't like Luke like that."

"I'm not telling you to marry him! Just go out and have some fun. Anyway, I'm going to bed," Powell announced, rising from his chair.

"Can I come with you?" Afina asked.

"I'm very tired. I need to get some sleep and I'm not sure you'd let me," Powell said lightly.

The last thing he wanted was to hurt Afina's feelings. In truth, he felt very confused about his own feelings. He definitely hadn't gotten over his experience with Lara. He had thought she was very special and the sex had been amazing, yet it had ended in disaster.

He had survived for many years with barely a special thought for any woman and never far from complete abstinence but recently his sexuality had definitely been reawakened. The result was he now couldn't understand his own emotions.

Since he'd been back, he was again feeling close to Afina but was it just a continuation of his growing physical desires? He knew the answer wasn't to go to bed with Afina. While it might be fun he had to treat her feelings with the greatest respect. He couldn't use her as a temporary means to satisfy his sexual desires and then move on when someone better came along. Not that he was even sure there would ever be anyone better. If he slept with her, he was quite sure she would take it as a sign they were in a relationship and he wasn't ready for a relationship.

Afina looked sad. "Have I done something wrong? I know you like me so why don't you want to make love to me?"

For a second, Powell was very tempted to change his mind. "I do like you, Afina but it's complicated. Just give me some time. Once all the problems with Gheorghe are out of the way, we can discuss this again." He leaned forward and kissed her on each cheek. "Good night."

CHAPTER FIFTY FIVE

Powell and Jenkins arrived at the Holiday Inn Hotel on the seafront, walked past reception as instructed and went directly to the lifts. They took the lift on the left and entered the code so the lift would take them to the eighth floor private apartments.

As they stepped out the lift, they noticed two men standing guard outside one of the apartments immediately became alert.

"We are here to see Gheorghe," Powell announced.

"Against the wall," one of the guards ordered.

Both men did as instructed and they were searched thoroughly for weapons. Then the guard knocked on the door and in the same movement opened it.

"You can go in," the guard said.

Powell entered, followed by Jenkins. The door opened onto a living room with further rooms leading off to either side. Two men quickly arose from their chairs and stared intently at the intruders.

"I'm Powell. Gheorghe is expecting us."

"He is coming," one of the men replied.

A minute later a man who fitted the description Afina had given of Gheorghe entered the room accompanied by a heavy set man on each shoulder.

"I am Gheorghe. Which of you is Powell?"

"I'm Powell."

"I assume you are also the man calling himself Danny?"

"Yes I am."

"So you are the man who killed my friends Dimitry and Victor, and put my son in jail."

Powell swallowed as his mouth was feeling a little dry. "They were responsible for the death of my daughter."

"So you decided it was okay to take revenge against my friends and family. You will learn that was not a wise decision but you asked for this meeting. What do you want?"

"I wanted to ask you to leave me and my bar alone. I also want you to promise no harm will come to Afina."

Gheorghe stared hard at Powell then burst into laughter. "You are a funny man. You come here with demands. I am still considering whether to let you leave here alive."

Jenkins stood straighter and cast his eyes around the room.

"You will rot in an English jail if we don't leave here within ten minutes, alive and well," Powell promised. "My friend Brian is very senior in the police and is waiting downstairs with a large number of colleagues, ready to arrest you all if we are harmed." Although it was a bluff, it seemed a logical explanation of the sensible precautions someone in his position would take.

"Bogdan tells me you are a very dangerous man. He warned me to be wary of you. And anyone who can do what you did to Dimitry and the others is undoubtedly dangerous but you are only human. You have a bar and friends like Afina, which makes you vulnerable. Why should I leave you alone?"

"It will save you a great deal of trouble. I have lost a daughter and your son is in jail. We are similarly suffering. You should return to your country or you will end up joining your son in prison."

"You know my business. I cannot maintain the respect of the people who work for me by doing nothing and running back home. You have to pay for what you have done."

Powell thought for a second about trying to end the trouble here and now but they were outnumbered five to two and there were probably more men, who would be armed, in the other rooms.

Powell's phone rang to break the tension in the room. He took it from his pocket and listened for a second. "No, it's okay. Stay down there. We will be down in a minute." He returned the phone to his pocket. The imaginary policeman downstairs was Afina.

"Time to be going," Powell announced. "Think about what I said."

"I have already and nothing has changed. I will kill you and give the bitch Afina to my men for sport. Now get out of here."

CHAPTER FIFTY SIX

Mara had confirmed she passed the details of Powell's celebration party to Gheorghe. She had an invite and was planning to attend. She had also informed Gheorghe that Afina would be attending.

Powell couldn't be certain Gheorghe would take the bait he'd dangled but he thought there was a significant chance the opportunity to spoil Powell's fun would be too difficult to resist.

The preparations were made and the bar was closed for the private party. It would cost Powell a significant sum in lost business but he could not risk having his regular customers in the bar when he expected trouble.

The guests started arriving at seven and were met inside the entrance to the bar by two doormen, one of whom was Jenkins, who checked they weren't members of the public straying into the wrong place. Powell hadn't wanted them to be isolated outside like normal doormen as they would be too exposed to attack from Gheorghe.

There were about thirty people in total in the bar. Food was laid out down one side of the room and free drinks were being served at the bar. Guests were standing around chatting. Afina was working behind the bar, serving drinks. As Powell surveyed the scene, he believed he had done everything possible for a good evening.

Powell observed Mara arrive. She went straight to the bar and ordered a glass of wine. He wandered over towards her, saying hello to a couple of people on the way.

"Hi Mara, it's good to see you. How are you?" Powell inquired.

"I'm good. Almost fully healed although I do have a souvenir scar. I'm thinking of getting it covered with a tattoo."

"Is everything organised?"

"Exactly as you wanted."

"Is what organised?" Afina asked, having overhead their conversation.

"Mara has invited some extra guests. What time are they expected?"

"At nine I am going to let them in through the fire escape at the back."

Powell was grateful to Mara and her acting skills. She had convinced

Gheorghe that she was on his side. Firstly, she had told him about the party and the fact it would be an opportunity to strike at Powell and Afina, at the same time.

Then Mara had explained she could get an invite and would help him get inside. The rear exit was by the toilets and she only had to agree a time when she would pretend to go to the toilets and instead would open the fire door.

Powell glanced at his watch. "One hour to go."

"What are you going to do when they get here?" Afina asked. "Should we tell your friends?"

"I'll wander around and warn everyone what to expect… Thanks for the help Mara."

Powell was keen to ensure Mara didn't look complicit in what was about to unfold. She had a mother back home and he didn't want her or anyone else being threatened by Gheorghe or his associates.

"Thank you, Powell. I've started to look for my own place by the way, and I'm going to do as you suggested."

"You're getting your own place?" Afina queried, surprised.

"I can't stay with Emma and Becky for ever and I need to start earning some money."

"I'm going to start circulating with the news," Powell said, wanting to leave Mara alone with Afina.

"What did Powell suggest?" Afina asked.

"He suggested, once my uncle was dealt with, I should get a nice flat and put my profile on a couple of adult sites."

"I don't understand? If your uncle is no longer a problem then why would you…" Afina stopped mid-sentence as she realised Mara's intention. "You are going to go back to work?"

"Yes, but working for myself. I am going to be a high class escort. It's what I want to do, Afina. Please don't give me your disapproving look."

"What disapproving look?"

"The one you always give at times like this." Mara gave an impersonation of Afina's disapproving face but in truth it was more comical than disapproving.

"I don't look like that!"

"Not quite like that maybe but you do scowl."

"Well Powell shouldn't be suggesting you continue whoring yourself."

"He asked me what I was going to do and I told him. He said that if I was intent on selling my body, I should do it with style, from a nice apartment and for good money."

"You make him sound like your pimp!"

"Afina, that isn't fair. Powell was simply trying to help and make sure I didn't end up working for someone else like my uncle. I've looked at the site he suggested and I can be an escort and do other things like cam shows. I will make good money."

"I'm sorry, we're just different."

"We are but that doesn't mean we can't still be friends. I've told Emma and Becky what I do, by the way."

"What did they say?"

"They were a bit shocked."

"To most people, it will be shocking."

"They weren't shocked by my selling my body, just that it's with men and not women."

"So they are still friends."

"Yes, but they did say they hoped I wasn't going to start charging them!"

Afina smiled and refilled their wine glasses.

"Are you still my friend?" Mara asked.

"I will always be your friend," Afina promised. "And just in case I ever want to have sex with you, I wish you to know I also won't expect to pay."

CHAPTER FIFTY SEVEN

Baz went to the apartment where not so long ago he had met with Lara and enjoyed her incredible body. Only a blind man would be immune to her beauty. It was her weapon, which she had used to entrap him but never had anyone been so happy to be caught in her web of deceit and lies.

He arrived early, as it would be extremely rude not to be there when his guest arrived. He made some tea and waited, knowing it could be a difficult meeting.

Baz had a text when his guest was one minute away, to warn him to have the door open so there would be no delay to him getting off the street and entering the apartment. Spending time in the open was not something this man did if it could possibly be avoided.

"May Allah's peace, mercy and blessing be upon you," Baz greeted his guest, shaking the man's hand and then kissing him on each cheek.

"And upon you peace."

Baz did not know the true name of his guest but knew him by his code name of Phoenix. An appropriate name for someone determined to see a new order in the Middle East, born of the ashes of war. He was older than Baz, probably in his late fifties, although his weathered skin made it difficult to be sure of his age.

Baz had heard that he had fought in more than his share of wars and his courage could not be questioned. But he was not just a fighter, he had a cunning mind and his specialty in his younger days, had been in planning devastating ambushes, which never left anyone alive. He was always merciless with his enemies. Now he was committed to planning the greatest attack on the West since 9/11.

Baz made his guest tea and they sat in the lounge. Baz had to shake his mind free of the images of Lara standing naked before him in the same room.

"I have to congratulate you," Phoenix said. "When you first approached me with your plan, I was not sure you would succeed but I believe your time spent living in England, has given you great insight into how our enemies think and behave, in a way that the rest of us can only pretend to understand."

"Thank you. Unfortunately, this knowledge did not extend to foreseeing the Englishman named Powell would return for a second time and take my children from under my nose."

"That is indeed unfortunate."

"I would like to try and bring back Karim. He had been showing great promise in his studies."

"I am not sure that is wise. We can achieve so much now you have been recruited by this devil that is called Lara."

"That is true but to have a boy born in England grow to manhood as a believer, able to go places and do things we can never achieve... The potential is enormous."

"I agree but it is important we do not draw attention to you. Lara would also not want this. She will dissuade you from any further attempt to recover your children."

"Perhaps if I bring back just Karim, my wife will be happy to have Laila and that will be the end of it. Then when Karim is about twenty we can send him back. He can pretend he has not been happy with me and wants to live in England. It will be an excellent cover story."

"Indeed it would but making it happen will not be easy. You risk exposing yourself and you are too valuable to put at risk, even for your son and the future he offers."

"I believe it is a risk we must take." Baz knew he must tread carefully. Phoenix was not a man used to having his authority challenged.

Phoenix was thoughtful. "You have served us very well and I would like to repay your service to our cause but your role in our next operation is vital. We will make the greatest ever strike against our accursed enemy and it is the information you will supply to Lara, which will make it possible."

"I understand but we are all exposed to risk every day of our lives. I could be killed in a traffic accident. I was almost killed by our own men at the Mall!"

"I am sorry about that. With hindsight I should have warned you to stay away but Allah was obviously looking out for you. He knows the great work you have to do in his name."

"I am sure you are right. Praise be to Allah."

"You yet again did a great service in providing the passports for our men to enter the country. Let me think further about what you say. For sure, you must do nothing for a few months. You must spend your time feeding information to Lara so you gain her trust. This is vital so she accepts the false information we will feed her next year. The planning for the operation is already advanced. Nothing must get in the way."

Baz realized he had to back off. Although what he said about the potential value of Karim to the cause was true, he was also speaking as a father. He wanted to see his son grow into manhood. He wanted to ensure his son was being taught correctly, which he would never be while living in England.

"I will abide by your wise decision, as always." Baz said, respectfully. "I have learned something of potential interest. She says that they have another person inside our organization, who can verify the information I provide. It may well be a bluff but…"

"I am sure they will have one or more of our men feeding them information but only at a low level. I have absolute confidence in everyone close to me and it is only those close to me that know anything significant."

"That is good to hear."

"So how is your relationship with Lara developing?"

"I am providing her with the information we agreed. I believe she is happy with me. I assume in the information I am providing, we are cleansing our organization of some unwanted elements?"

"We will be happy to see the back of one or two of the names on your list but there are also some we are sacrificing to enhance your credibility. Never forget that men will die, quite possibly in agony, for helping you to gain the trust of this woman. "

"I understand and I will not fail you." Baz understood his role and the information he was to provide, would be pivotal in the success of the massive operation being planned but he had no idea what the information was. He would only learn that at the appropriate time. He was excited to know that he had such an important role to play in the greatest ever strike against the west.

"I am sure you will not fail us. You have always done everything we asked of you. You were even willing to allow yourself to be trapped by the devil that is this woman called Lara. That is not something every man would be willing to suffer."

Baz thought he detected a slight smile on the lips of Phoenix. He had seen Lara and knew she was beautiful.

"It was my duty," Baz acknowledged. He was actually thinking it may have been his duty but it was also a memorable experience. If only all duty was so pleasant. He had spent too many years in England doing his duty.

Despite his absolute commitment to restoring the true Islam to the world, he recognized his personal failings. One of his biggest weaknesses was his attraction to beautiful women. Even if they were non-believers they still offered the possibility of memorable, momentary pleasure. He looked forward to his seventy two virgins in heaven and he would not be short of ideas or the experience of how to enjoy them.

He hoped one day in the future to experience further the pleasures of Lara's flesh. Maybe he would pretend to waver in his commitment and she would be prepared to offer him her body again. He smiled at the thought. What fools these westerners were and so predictable. They believe themselves to be superior but everything about them is superficial.

It had been relatively easy to set in motion the events leading to his falling into what she believed was her trap but it was he who had truly set the trap. He had lured her in with his flirting at the embassy parties and made it obvious he found her attractive.

He had known she would want to snare him and when she accepted his invitation to meet at the apartment, he expected there to be a sting in the tail.

"Be careful with this woman," Phoenix warned. "She is not to be underestimated."

"I will be careful. I will play the role of her puppet for many months but when it matters we will be pulling the strings."

Phoenix arose to signal the meeting was at an end. "We will meet again in two weeks as usual. Go in peace my friend."

CHAPTER FIFTY EIGHT

At five minutes to nine Powell was feeling tense. He'd already tried to convince Afina she should go upstairs to the flat, where she would be safer, but he might as well have tried to convince a nun to have sex. She was adamant she was going nowhere but pointed out she had the bar for cover. She certainly didn't lack courage but even behind the bar, she was still exposed to danger and he could not imagine how he would cope with the guilt, if something happened to her.

For now though, he needed to focus on Gheorghe and his friends. Mara thought he had about eight men staying with him. Powell didn't want to see anyone harmed and if Gheorghe brought all of his men with him, it could turn into a bloodbath, one of Powell's making.

Mara looked at him and gave a slight nod as she moved towards the toilets and fire escape. He looked across to the bar and gave Afina a reassuring smile.

Powell was counting on Gheorghe wanting to savour his moment not rush in all guns blazing. He didn't expect anyone at the party to offer resistance or be armed but Powell had his trusty weapon, which had tamed Victor, in the back of his trouser belt.

All at once, there was a change in the party atmosphere as Gheorghe and several others rushed into the room waving their weapons at everyone and shouting for them to get on the floor. There was general pandemonium as guests complained at being pushed around and others were shouted at for being too slow to react. Powell remained standing as the gang spread out and ensured everyone was on the floor. Gheorghe approached him with a self-satisfied smile.

"I guess you might as well remain standing," Gheorghe said. "Did you really think I would allow you to celebrate my son's imprisonment and the death of my friends?"

"This is a private party," Powell said coolly. "And you weren't invited."

Powell was pleased there was no sign of Mara. He had instructed her, once she had opened the rear exit, to leave so she could always deny any knowledge of what took place later. She had done her bit by opening the door and hopefully no one back in Romania would have cause to suspect she knew it was a trap.

"Where is Afina," Gheorghe asked, casting his eyes around the bar. He recognised Afina standing behind the bar. "I know you. You are the girl from the hospital." A knowing smile crossed his face. "So you are Afina. Come over here."

Gheorghe studied Afina as she walked towards him. "My men are going to enjoy playing with you." He slapped her hard around the face as soon as she stood before him, knocking her to the ground. Even as he did it, he raised his gun and pointed it at Powell's chest, knowing his action might evoke a reaction. "That is for your lack of respect at the hospital."

Afina was on the floor, glaring at Gheorghe. "You don't deserve respect. You're a pig."

Gheorghe smiled. "Take off all your clothes. Let's see what you look like naked and then my men can teach you a proper lesson while all these people watch."

"Okay this has gone far enough," Powell stated in an even voice. "Gheorghe, I want you and your men to lay down your weapons."

Gheorghe looked incredulous. "Or you will do what?" He turned to his men. "Do you hear that, he wants us to lay down our weapons." The men all laughed.

"If you don't lay your weapons down now, you will all end up dead."

"Have you gone mad. I will give the orders and I am telling this bitch to take off her clothes."

"This is my party you have gate-crashed and Afina is not part of the entertainment. Look around the room at my friends and what do you notice?"

Gheorghe stopped laughing and glanced to his right. He immediately swept around the room to see that every one of the guests had a weapon in their hand.

"Put down your weapons or you will all end up dead. These are my friends. They are all present or former soldiers. We are over thirty guns and you have just six."

Gheorghe again raised his weapon and pointed it at Powell's chest. "If someone is going to die tonight, you will be the first."

"Nobody has to die but make no mistake, if one of you fires a single shot, my men will kill all of you. There will be no second chance to surrender."

Powell could see some of Gheorghe's men were looking very uncomfortable. They were casting nervous glances in all directions, knowing they were hopelessly outnumbered.

"We are not the sort of men you can so easily intimidate," Gheorghe responded. He pointed his gun at Afina. "Tell your men to put down their weapons or I will kill this bitch."

Powell looked behind Gheorghe's shoulder and made a tiny, almost imperceptible movement with his eyes. Gheorghe caught the movement and started to turn. As he did so, Powell used the lightning reflexes honed over many years to punch him crisply on the nose.

Gheorghe teetered but before he could regain his balance, Powell had moved in sideways, gripped his arm holding the gun and then thrown him over his shoulder to the floor. It was a move he had practised a thousand times before on the mat where he trained. In training it was a pure throw to the mat but this time Powell held on to the wrist as Gheorghe hit the ground, enabling him to bend the arm backwards with the result he was able to easily prise the weapon from Gheorghe's grip, as he threatened to break his arm. Powell took a step back and aimed the weapon at Gheorghe before he had barely had time to register the first punch.

"Put down your weapons," Powell shouted.

The soldiers were climbing to their feet and moving to each Romanian in turn, as he put down his weapon. Each man had his hands put behind their back in handcuffs and was then pushed to the floor. Within a minute the danger had been nullified.

Afina had climbed to her feet and looked down at Gheorghe. "You are pure evil," she said, angrily. "You think it is okay to buy and sell girls like me. You are an apology for a man."

"Fuck you," Gheorghe swore.

"I remember saying that to Stefan, the first night I arrived in England. He laughed, then both he and Dimitry raped me. They are not laughing now. And no one will be fucking you for a very long time unless of course the inmates of your prison take a fancy to you."

Afina walked away towards the bar, picked up her glass of wine and took a large drink. Powell phoned the police and explained briefly what had happened. Then he joined Afina at the bar and poured himself a shot of whisky, which he downed in one.

"You okay?" he asked.

"They make me so angry. How do they become such monsters?"

"I think some men are just born bad. Maybe it's their upbringing but once they are adults they make their own choices so we shouldn't make excuses for them."

"Tell me Powell, why did you organise this party and everything the way you did? It was dangerous. People could have been killed."

"Everyone here was aware of the danger and volunteered. Most of them are current or former soldier friends of Jenkins. Many of them are also fathers and once they realised Gheorghe's crimes against young women, were more than happy to take the risk. We needed incontrovertible proof of their guilt and witnesses who will not be intimidated when they stand in the witness box. Everything that happened has been captured on our CCTV. I was told if we could do this, there would be enough evidence to charge them all with attempted murder, which will ensure a very long prison sentence. Hopefully, it will also put an end to their trafficking girls into Brighton."

"Thank you, Powell. I am once again in your debt."

"You owe me nothing, Afina. Without you I would never have been able to find Bella's killers."

Jenkins joined them at the bar. "I wouldn't say no to a whisky."

Powell pored a large whisky and handed it to Jenkins.

Jenkins downed it in one. "Fuck, you can move fast," he said. "Never seen anything like that... Except of course in a Bruce Lee movie. Now that man could really kick ass."

"You should come training with me," Powell suggested. "You both should. It's a great way of keeping fit."

"I'd like to try it," Afina replied. "I need to learn how to defend myself."

"I'll give it a go," Jenkins agreed.

Police sirens could be heard approaching.

Afina smiled. "You know, I like the name Powell but one day I hope you are going to tell me your first name."

"Not a chance. My parents were sixties hippies. They had strange ideas of what made a suitable name for a boy."

THE END

Trafficking
Powell Book 1

Trafficking is big business and those involved show no remorse, have no mercy, only a deadly intent to protect their income.

Afina is a young Romanian girl with high expectations when she arrives in Brighton but she has been tricked and there is no job, only a life as a sex slave.

Facing a desperate future, Afina tries to escape and a young female police officer, who comes to her aid, is stabbed.

Powell's life has been torn apart for the second time and he is determined to find the man responsible for his daughter's death.

Action, violence and sex abound in this taut thriller about one of today's worst crimes.

5* reviews

"This book is not for the faint hearted but it is a brilliant read."

"Keeps you at the edge of your seat throughout."

"Exciting, terrifying, brilliant."

"One of the best books I have read in a long time!"

"Will leave you breathless."

REVENGE.

There is no greater motivator for evil than a huge sense of injustice!

Tom Ashdown, an unlikely hero, owns a betting shop in Brighton and gambles with his life when he stumbles across an attempted kidnapping, which leaves him entangled in a dangerous chain of events involving the IRA, a sister seeking revenge for the death of her brother and an informer in MI5 with a secret in his past.

Revenge is a fast paced thriller, with twists and turns at every step.

In a thrilling and violent climax everyone is intent on some form of revenge.

5* Reviews

"Fast paced from the start and it only goes faster!"

"This novel is a real page turner!"

"It will keep you on the edge of your seat."

"Revenge is an example of everything that I look for in an action thriller."

ENCRYPTION.

In a small software engineering company in England, a game changing algorithm for encrypting data has been invented, which will have far reaching consequences for the fight against terrorism.

The Security Services of the UK, USA and China all want to control the new software.

The Financial Director has been murdered and his widow turns to her brother-in-law to help discover the truth. But he soon finds himself framed for his brother's murder.

When the full force of government is brought to bear on one family, they seem to face impossible odds. Is it an abuse of power or does the end justify the means?

Only one man can find the answers but he is being hunted by the same people he once called friends and colleagues.

5* Reviews

"A Great English Spy Thriller."

"This is a great story! Once I started reading it, I could not put it down."

"A superior read in a crowded genre!"

"Full of memorable characters and enough twists and turns to impress all diehard thriller junkies, it is a wonderful read"

"If you're a fan of Ludlum, and love descriptive prose like that of Michener, you'll be right at home."

ABOUT THE AUTHOR

Bill Ward lives in Brighton with his German partner Anja. He has recently retired from senior corporate roles in large IT companies and is now following a lifelong passion for writing! With 7 daughters, a son, stepson, 2 horses, a dog, 2 cats and 2 Guinea pigs, life is always busy!

Bill's other great passion is supporting West Bromwich Albion, which he has been doing for more than 50 years!

Buy all Bill's books at all leading online stores including:
amazon.com/Bill-Ward/e/B00F154DZ2/re
amazon.co.uk/Bill-Ward/e/B00F154DZ2/re

Connect with Bill online:

Twitter: http://twitter.com/billward10bill

Facebook: http://facebook.com/billwardbooks